WINTER'S GIFTS

WINTER'S GIFTS

BEN AARONOVITCH

ORION

First published in Great Britain in 2022 by Orion Fiction,
an imprint of The Orion Publishing Group Ltd.,
Carmelite House, 50 Victoria Embankment
London EC4Y 0DZ

An Hachette UK Company

1 3 5 7 9 10 8 6 4 2

A CIP catalogue record for this book is
available from the British Library.

ISBN (Hardback) 978 1 473 22437 7
ISBN (eBook) 978 1 473 22439 1

Typeset by Input Data Services Ltd, Somerset

Printed and bound in Great Britain by Clays Ltd, Elcograf S.p.A.

www.orionbooks.co.uk

For Sabrina and Andreas, for always being there when I needed them.

Proprium humani ingenii est odisse quem laeseris.
It belongs to human nature to hate those you have injured.

Publius Cornelius Tacitus

1

On the afternoon of September 11th 2001, my mama called me at my dorm and begged me not to join the Marines. Up until that phone call I had, like most of my dorm mates, spent the day staring at the TV in stunned disbelief. But my mama was already thinking ahead to the war she was sure was coming, and she didn't want my brother, who was a high school freshman at the time, getting it into his head to enlist.

I tell myself that no doubt Mama recognised that I was too sensible to get myself killed in a foreign war, and sometimes I even believe it.

She made me swear on my Bible, which I hadn't even unpacked yet.

I prayed to Jesus for guidance that night and he must have comforted me, because I fell asleep in the early hours and the next week I went back to classes. Once the shock had worn off, I, like most other folk, went back to my life as normal.

I think it might surprise a lot of people that the majority of FBI agents don't graduate high school, or even college, planning to join the Bureau. That's because the FBI likes its recruits to be what in modern management-speak is called 'self-directed', or what my mama calls 'grown-ups'. They want you to have an education and life experience first and, best of all, they want you to have skills they can put to use. Right now if you want to join the FBI, try working in STEM first. They'll eat that up.

I majored in Healthcare Administration but minored in Criminal Justice. I'd taken Theories of Criminal Behaviour in my second semester because I'd wanted to know why a bunch of well-educated young men might want to fly a plane into the side of a building, and I guess that sparked my interest.

I was recruited out of college by a health insurance company, which was my career plan, into their fraud investigation division, and from there, a hop, skip and a jump to running an investigation team for an agricultural insurance company. I had my own office and a reserved space in the company parking lot.

But it all started to feel kind of petty.

Also, my mama got it into her head that I was persecuting decent, honest hard-working folk on behalf of the liberal corporate elite. She hadn't discovered the word 'woke' yet, and I'm never going to forgive my brother for bringing it to her attention. I should have let him join the Air Force like he threatened to. Now he's a minister in Mama's church and can do no wrong.

My decision to apply to be a special agent crept up on me some time between the case of the spontaneously exploding tractor and the cows that ate Paris, Arkansas.

I told my mama that Jesus led me to join the FBI, and when she asked why I told her I didn't think it was right to question the Lord. She gave me a funny look – never think people like my mama are stupid – but she also cooked me a peach cobbler that couldn't be beat and gave me her blessing.

Who knows, Jesus might have spoken in my heart, in which case London, magic, the talking bears and everything else were also part of his design. After all, ever since I was a little girl my mama has told me that God is constantly sending us messages, only sometimes we let the noise of our everyday lives get in the way of hearing them. She says that we have to let Jesus be the switchboard operator of our souls and always be ready to take his call.

But I believe even Jesus would have his work cut out dealing with the thousands of unsolicited calls that arrive at the Bureau's main switchboard every day. Of these, a small but significant number ask to be put through to *The X-Files*. All these calls are logged, recorded and reviewed, even the ones from people who believe that the Federal Government is being run by space lizards. Perhaps especially those ones. Just in case the caller is the kind of crazy who's sitting on two tons of fertiliser-based IED and looking for an excuse to use it.

Still, winnowing the wheat from the chaff takes time. And so it wasn't until Monday morning that the message from former agent Patrick Henderson arrived as an email on the secure terminal in my cubicle at the Critical Incident Response Group. The email was from Jan – who was PA to my boss Lane Harris, assistant director CIRG – inviting me to a meeting in his office at 9:30. A transcript of the telephone message was added as an attachment for reference.

Given that the meeting was in fifteen minutes, the transcript was mercifully short. Having reached a human operator, the caller immediately identified himself as Patrick Henderson, resident of Eloise, Wisconsin and a former FBI agent.

OPERATOR: How can I help you, Mr. Henderson?

CALLER: I need you to pass a message to whoever is running the basement and tell them that we have a potential X-RAY SIERRA INDIA developing. I'll advise in person when they get here.

OPERATOR: I'm sorry, sir, but I'm not sure—

CALLER: You won't understand what any of this means, ma'am. Just pass it up the chain until somebody does.

Patrick Henderson then gives his home address, in Eloise, his landline and a cell number. Before he hangs up he says one more thing:

CALLER: This is important, we need an assessment right away.

I had enough time to confirm that Patrick Henderson was indeed a former agent who'd retired early at 42. Most agents start their FBI careers in their early thirties and retiring early means missing out on much of your pension. Digging deeper, I found that Henderson had retired due to ill health, although no details were given as to what the problem was. The files confirmed his address as Eloise, a small town in northern Wisconsin, population 521, famous for fishing, tourism

4

and the winter ice road to the Apostle Islands National Lakeshore.

Before I left for the meeting, I searched for X-RAY SIERRA INDIA and found no references internally and nothing on Google.

The 'basement' reference I already knew about. It was the unofficial name used inside the Bureau to refer to my 'department'. It was a throwback to the aforementioned TV show *The X-Files*, where the heroes worked out of a basement in the J. Edgar Hoover Building, combating aliens, supernatural creatures and monsters.

In truth, I work for the IOSS, the Investigative and Operations Support Section of the Critical Incident Response Group. One of many special assistants to the assistant director who runs the section.

Still, Patrick Henderson's reference to 'the basement' intrigued me. He'd retired in 1999, which implied that someone had been doing my job almost a decade before I'd joined the FBI. I wondered where their files were being stored, because I'd never seen them.

Since my cubicle was down the hall from the assistant director's office, there was no excuse to be late, and so I made sure I presented myself outside his door at 9:29.

Jan looked up from their terminal and, after eyeing me curiously over their horn-rimmed glasses for a moment, waved me into the office. They didn't follow me in, which was unusual. Usually, Jan takes notes even at routine meetings.

Assistant Director Lane Harris looked like a well-dressed accountant in his mid-fifties. His hairline had long receded all the way back to the nape of his neck, leaving two wings of greying brown hair, cut short, on either side. They gave him somewhat the appearance of a cartoon owl. He had a straight nose, small blue eyes, thin lips, and looked like he should be wearing little round-framed glasses but wasn't. His office had that half-furnished utilitarian look that most senior managers' offices at Quantico have, with standard institutional coffee-coloured carpeting, wood panelling on two of the walls, and sturdy wooden bookcases lining the rest. He had a window overlooking the parking lot but I noticed that the baffle curtains, designed to stop anyone eavesdropping with a laser microphone, had been pulled across to cover the window.

He was standing behind his metal-framed desk when I entered.

'Kimberley,' he said. 'Have a seat.'

As we sat down opposite each other, he leaned back in his chair and clasped his fingers across his belly.

'What's your first question?' he asked.

'What does "X-Ray Sierra India" indicate?'

Harris nodded – obviously this was the right question.

'It's an old case designation that dates back to the 1990s,' he said. 'I've never encountered it myself, but it's fairly well known – or was. It indicates that the agent compiling the file believes that the case might have some unusual characteristics.'

'Unusual characteristics', or UC, was the Bureau's euphemism for the weird, the supernatural and the genuine occult. Unusual characteristics was my current assignment and, I was beginning to fear, a forecast for my future career.

'What does it stand for?' I asked.

'I have no idea,' said Harris. 'But it's only supposed to be used for serious situations. You've had a look at Patrick Henderson's file. Do you think he's credible?'

I said that I would have preferred to know how he came to be medically retired, but from what I'd read he'd had an unremarkable though solid career in the Bureau. And there was no record of him making frivolous calls to us in the past, so I was tempted to give him the benefit of the doubt.

'That was my assessment, too,' said Harris.

'I think we should at least find out what he's got to say,' I said.

Harris nodded. We were both aware that there were worrying gaps in the files where they related to 'unusual circumstances'. The FBI was in the information business, and the idea that cases had been removed did not sit well with either of us.

'He seems to expect us to send someone up,' said Harris.

Important, Henderson had said. *We need an assessment right away.*

'If we're going to take him seriously,' I said, 'then let's take him seriously. I could fly up tomorrow – make an "assessment". If there is an ongoing UC then I'll be on the ground to make further recommendations.'

Harris nodded.

'At the very least,' he said. 'Since our records are regrettably incomplete, it would be useful to have a source with "basement" experience to help fill in the blanks.'

Sources are important. The FBI prides itself on being an intelligence-led organisation. Agents are evaluated as much on the quantity and quality of their key sources as they are on their criminal case files. Harris has been pitching for more resources, but until senior management starts to take the supernatural seriously we go with what we can get.

Fortunately, Washington is as much a magnet for weirdos as Los Angeles. I'd found some useful intelligence assets since being assigned to what my mama calls 'the nation's cesspit'. Mama is not a fan of the Federal Government, although she makes an exception for the military, the Post Office and, more recently, Medicare.

Cymbeline Moonglum – that's the name on her birth certificate, by the way, I looked it up – shared my mama's suspicion of the Feds, but for diametrically opposed political reasons. She worked for an environmental advocacy group near McPherson Square, and I call her an intelligence asset because the Bureau doesn't approve of agents putting *inveterate gossip* on their expenses claims. She also used to be a witch – a real one – so as soon as I got back to my desk, I called her and arranged to have lunch.

'If I'd known the FBI was paying,' said Cymbeline, 'I'd have chosen a swankier spot.'

We were in a coffee shop on 14th Street, having just managed to grab one of the stripped pine tables for ourselves, despite the lunchtime crowd that steamed up the windows. It was the kind of place that served avocado toast, and your coffee arrived in its own press with a little card describing the country of origin and how it was ethically sourced. They did manage to serve a good quarter-pounder without adding either kale or quinoa – but you could tell they really wanted to.

And it was plenty expensive enough by my standards, thank you very much.

'This comes out of my pocket first,' I said.

Cymbeline Moonglum was in her late thirties, tall, and ridiculously thin given how she was scarfing her cheeseburger and fries. She was dressed like any other Washington lifer in a navy-blue skirt suit and pink blouse, except for the Celtic knot pendant she wore on a silver chain. Power clung to that pendant. I know because I've been taught to sense what those in the know call *vestigia* – the traces that are left behind by magic.

Cymbeline hovered her hand over my fries.

'May I?' she asked.

'Help yourself,' I said. She helped herself. 'What do you know about Wisconsin?'

'Terrible problem with water contamination,' she said. 'Particularly PFOS from landfill run-off. Persistent, toxic, and it bioaccumulates – don't go swimming in any lakes.'

'What else?' I asked.

'More cougar sightings,' she said. 'Which is encouraging.'

We played this game every single time we met. I don't know why, except Cymbeline seemed to get some weird

9

satisfaction from making me wait. Which I was content to do, seeing as I knew she was as desperate to tell me the latest gossip as I was to hear it.

'More to the point, it might be interesting to you,' said Cymbeline. 'There have been rumours that the animal spirits are returning.'

'Like these cougars?' I said, and pulled my fries away from her minatory fingers.

'Probably not the cougars,' she said. 'But an old friend of mine in New Hampshire ...' The stress she put on the words 'old friend' indicated that she was talking about a fellow witch. 'They said that there were indications that some of the bears there might be manifestations.'

Manifestations was Cymbeline-speak for the spirit or god of a locality. What my British colleague Peter Grant would call a *genius loci* – which is just a fancy way of saying 'local spirit'.

'She says that there are clear indications that other bears defer to them,' she said. 'Perhaps even some of the local people, too. They leave out offerings and in return their crops and animals prosper.' According to Cymbeline, similar spirits were popping up all across North America. 'Wherever the population density is low. And trust me, you don't want to fucking mess with them.'

I must have winced or something, because Cymbeline laughed.

'I can't believe you work for the FBI,' she said. 'Or don't the bad guys say "fuck" anymore?'

'I just don't like cursing, OK,' I said. 'It's unnecessary.'

'How about blaspheming?'

But I've had that particular argument – about paganism, Christianity and what Cymbeline calls my outrageous double standards – before, so I steered her back to *genii locorum* and *manifestations*.

'Anything specific to Wisconsin?' I asked.

'Apart from the cougars?'

'Apart from the talking animals.'

'Who said they were talking?'

I pushed my fries back toward Cymbeline, who smiled and took them.

'Why, Agent Reynolds, do you really think you can bribe me with your leftover deep-fried potato snacks?' she said.

'Wisconsin,' I said.

'Nothing recently,' said Cymbeline as she finished the fries. 'I've heard stories from the old days, you know, when it was the frontier.'

There were stories of clashes between British magical practitioners and Native American medicine men during the War of 1812, although Cymbeline was hazy both about who was fighting who and just when Wisconsin became a state. I have to admit that I'd had to spend half an hour on the internet reading up on the history myself. What was part of the Northwest Territory became in sequence, in the space of half a century, part of the Indiana, Illinois and Michigan territories before becoming its own territory in 1836 and a state in 1848. The town of Eloise wasn't officially founded until the 1850s, sandwiched between Bayfield to the south and the Red Cliff Reservation to the north.

'There's rumours that an expedition by the Virgins went missing up there,' said Cymbeline. 'I can't remember when that was supposed to be. Would you like me to ask around?'

'If you could,' I said.

'The Virgins' was witchspeak for the Virginia Gentlemen's Company, who had been founded by none other than Thomas Jefferson himself. Just like the Pinkertons had served as an unofficial intelligence and national police force, the VGC had served as the magical arm of the US Government.

'I heard the Virgins got their asses handed to them in London,' said Cymbeline.

'That's what I heard,' I said shading the truth.

Actually, I'd been sent over to repatriate their sorry asses back to Virginia. I'd been hoping the Brits would prosecute them, but they, in the form of Peter Grant, said they couldn't be bothered.

More likely, they didn't want to admit that full-scale magical warfare had broken out on the streets of London.

'They used to be real wizards,' said Cymbeline. 'Now they're just corporate.'

The malign influence of creeping corporatisation was one of Cymbeline's hobby horses and, to head her off, I asked whether she knew any details about the Virginians' missing expedition.

'I know it was on Lake Superior because they travelled up by boat,' she said. 'They set out from Sault Sainte Marie – wait, I've remembered it was definitely eighteen forty-something, if that helps – and never came back.'

'That's it?'

'I'm not sure it's even true,' she said.

'Why not?'

'Because it was supposed to be a big expedition, with boats, horses, scouts and native guides,' she said. 'You'd think by now somebody would have found some trace of them. Expeditions that big don't just disappear.'

2

I flew into MSP the next morning and picked up a Toyota 4Runner as the available model least likely to get blown off the highway. It was cold and bright and I was wearing sunglasses against the glare until Spooner. There I stopped for coffee and a pretty decent po' boy at an eccentric little roadside restaurant that had a stuffed black bear guarding the service counter. In the half hour I was there, the weather closed in and it began to snow.

Highway 63 was cleared and gritted and the Toyota had all-weather tyres, so despite increasingly heavy snow I kept at a steady 50 and only had one scare when an idiot in a Chevy Malibu overtook, lost control and put himself on the shoulder. I slowed just in case he needed assistance, but he was soon out of his car and looking sorrowful in my rear-view mirror.

After lunch with Cymbeline, I'd spent the afternoon arranging to meet Special Agent Sean Doughty, out of the Wausau Field Office, who agreed to drive up and meet me at Eloise.

'Make sure you bring your cold weather gear with you,' he'd said. 'There's a severe weather warning listed for the Red Cliffs and Bayfield.'

Which might explain why both Patrick Henderson and the Eloise PD's landlines went straight to voicemail. I contacted the Bayfield County Sheriff, who informed me that the lines had gone down because of heavy snow and assured me this wasn't unusual for January.

When I turned onto the two-lane highway that ran up the lake shore, I found out what they meant. The snow was moderate but relentless and visibility dropped to a hundred feet, and I slowed the heck down. By the time I reached Bayfield I was running behind schedule and couldn't afford anything more than a coffee and a comfort break before pushing on.

The land rose abruptly on the other side of Bayfield, the highway climbing steeply up to a saddle between two hills. The road couldn't have been ploughed more than half a day previous, but it was already vanishing under fresh snow and I was glad to have the four-wheel drive on the steeper sections.

Visibility was down to twenty feet as I came over the ridge, so I was spared what the town's website called a picturesque panorama. Eloise Point, which the town was presumably named after, unless it was vice versa, failed to rear majestically at the north end of the harbour. All I could see was snow and even more snow with every passing moment.

The main street into town had been recently ploughed, and I saw the residential streets had been ploughed and buried again in the snow. Fortunately, they grit early in northern Wisconsin, and keep gritting and ploughing with grim determination, no matter what. I followed the cleared roads down a gentle slope to the waterfront and turned left toward where my satnav said that Eloise PD shared a building with the rest of the town's civil administration.

The building was gone.

Later I found out that the town hall had been a one-storey brick building, simple and sturdy. I've seen buildings levelled by bombs, runaway trucks and what we're officially calling an atypical sinkhole formation. But this one shouted 'tornado'. I didn't know you could even get tornados in winter, but nothing says tornado like brick walls being knocked flat all of a piece.

I said a little prayer for whoever had been in there when that happened. The last update I'd had reported that the chief and all his deputies were still listed as un-available. But if they'd been in the building, why wasn't it swarming with emergency response teams?

A man in a heavy blue parka and a reflective orange vest was taking photographs in front of what was left of the town hall.

Despite the cold, he had the hood of his parka thrown back to reveal thick black hair pulled back into a pony-tail, a handsome narrow face and a dark complexion.

He turned when he heard the Toyota approach and held up his hand in a stopping motion and pointed to the ground in front of the car. I stopped and got out. Where he'd been pointing was a section of some white material with splintered edges. I realised with a shock I was looking at the side of a small sailboat that had been lifted up and smashed down on the road. Once I knew what to look for, I saw other debris half-hidden by the snow.

Not something I'd have wanted to drive into, or over. The Bureau does not like to lose its deposit.

I waited as the man picked his way through the debris toward me. I was wearing my parka, but I was suddenly aware that I hadn't changed into my thermals, boots or even put on my gloves. The still air was freezing – if a wind came up, it would be dangerously cold.

'Are you the Fed?' he asked. 'Pat said that they were sending a Fed all the way from Washington.'

I told him I was Special Agent Reynolds of the FBI and left it at that. I did wonder who Pat was. The man stretched out a gloved hand for me to shake.

'William Boyd,' he said. 'Meteorologist. I'm up from Madison to study the weird weather. But don't worry, I'm not a hobbit.'

He smiled as if awaiting a response, but it was a mystery to me as to what.

'Who's Pat?' I asked.

'Deputy Patricia Larson,' said Boyd. 'From the county sheriff's office in Washburn. She's manning the emergency centre.'

'You couldn't tell me where that is?' I had to shout as a freezing wind off the lake suddenly blew up around us.

Boyd pointed off to the left at what might have been a parking lot.

'Over there!' he shouted back.

I got back in the car and, with Boyd walking ahead of me, pulled into the shelter of a large nearby boathouse. Part of the concrete apron was shielded by a row of linked open-fronted sheds and was currently serving as a garage. At one end was a bright orange backhoe with chained wheels and a snowplough attachment, next to that was a white Ford Explorer in County Sheriff's logo. I parked my rental in between that and a Ford F150 that looked like it had been rolled at least twice in its eventful lifetime.

I took the time to change into my boots. I hadn't worn them for at least three years, and they creaked a bit as I pulled them on over the thick wool socks Mama insists on sending me every Christmas. After a moment's hesitation, I also pulled on the matching woollen stocking cap, from the same Christmas care package, and pulled it down so it covered my ears. I hate cold ears.

I glanced out and saw that Boyd was standing beyond the shelter and squinting up at the sky, snow falling onto his upturned face. All I could see were the heavy blue-grey clouds that seemed to scrape the tops of the nearby buildings. I made a mental note to change into my thermals at the first opportunity, and climbed out of the Toyota. At least the wind had dropped again.

'Do you know what happened?' I asked Boyd when I joined him.

'Ice tornado,' he said. 'Came in off the lake early this morning around 7:15.'

I looked back at the remains of the city offices.

'I didn't know you got tornadoes in winter,' I said.

Boyd grinned – he had an infectious grin.

'They're astonishingly rare,' he said. 'By rights, there shouldn't be enough energy in the environment to create the right conditions. And there wasn't any sign of a supercell on the satellite images.'

A gust of wind caught us and my nose went numb. His, too, I figured, because he nodded over to a solid-looking building beside the boathouse.

'We'd better get inside,' he said.

Boyd led me toward the large high-roofed barn of a building. It seemed completely undamaged, despite being less than twenty feet from the town hall. Opening a side door, he ushered me into an interior that didn't seem much warmer than the outside. There was what looked like the hull of a big boat under dirty orange tarpaulins against one wall. In the centre of the room, some trestle tables had been set up on which neat piles of gear, including half a dozen shotguns and a walkie-talkie recharger, were neatly laid out. A liquid propane space heater sat facing a line of folding chairs that had been draped with wet clothes that steamed and filled the room with the smell of damp wool. Spare LP tanks were lined up by the shrouded boat, a good safe distance from the heater or any other fire source. A young woman in a county deputy's sheriff's uniform, with a clipboard, was checking supplies and making notes.

'Pat,' called Boyd, and the woman turned. She had blonde hair plaited into a sensible French braid and blue eyes, and looked like she should be trying out for her high school cheerleading team. Her face lit up in a delighted smile when she saw us.

'Mr. Bear,' she said.

'Boyd,' said Boyd. 'And this is Special Agent Reynolds.'

'Deputy Patricia Larson,' said Patricia and stuck out her hand to shake. She was wearing thin glove liners made of smooth stretchy fabric. I was immediately envious of them and wished I'd thought to buy a pair for myself.

'Kimberley,' I said.

'Bill,' said Boyd.

'Billy,' said Patricia, ignoring Boyd's sigh, 'Washburn called and said that the 13 is closed at Princes Ridge and south of the Red Cliffs.'

Boyd looked at me.

'You must have been one of the last people to get through,' he said,

Chances were Agent Doughty was stuck on the other side. Certainly, when I asked, Patricia said I was the only Fed they'd seen.

'Is the police chief around?' I asked. 'He wasn't . . . ?' I gestured in the direction of the flattened town hall.

'No, thank God,' said Patricia. 'There was nobody inside at the time, but a hell of thing, though. You think you've seen everything the lake can throw at you and then . . .' She shrugged. 'The chief is out with Henry and Gottlieb, checking on the houses that got wrecked.'

'Does he need any help?' I asked.

'Nah,' said Patricia. 'They've got it handled.'

The cell service was intermittent, but the landlines running south had been temporarily patched so I called Quantico and told them I was stuck. Jan promised to let their boss know and call the Wausau office to update them on my status.

That done, I checked my watch. Even with the over-cast I had at least another hour of daylight left. I asked Patricia for directions to Henderson's address.

'Two blocks over,' she said. 'Then left up the hill for two blocks.'

I thanked her and, since I had a meteorologist on hand, I asked Boyd whether it was going to get much colder.

He gave it some thought.

'Probably,' he said. 'I'm definitely expecting more snow.'

'In that case,' I said to Patricia, 'is there somewhere I can change?'

When I unpacked my thermals, they had that musty smell that even clean clothes get if you leave them in the closet for five years. I made sure to tuck everything in. Even when I was assigned to the field office in Albany, where we had proper winters, I mostly drove between heated buildings, but I remembered the times I'd been caught outside in a light jacket and office slacks.

While I was changing, somebody must have taken the tractor with the snowplough attachment out and cleared a path from the shelter to the road. I followed the wide swath it had pushed through the freshly fallen snow until the track turned left at the end of the block. According to the map I'd downloaded while I still had cell coverage, that was Holloway Avenue, the town's main drag. Obviously they'd want to clear that first. I considered following it and zigzagging to Henderson's address, but the wind had dropped and the snow had been replaced by a light fog, glittering a milky white. Visibility was down to fifteen feet, but the Toyota was still getting a good grip on the road, so I kept going.

I took the third left on to John Adams Avenue. The slope quickly grew steeper, but the tyres were new and I maintained my momentum until the slope levelled off some. I topped a ridge and saw the corner where Henderson had his house. It was a one-storey ranch house with steep roofs and a separate garage. No lights were visible as I pulled up outside and got out and looked around.

The house next door was a flat shadow softened by the fog. There was a yellow glow from a window, and I could hear the distinctive tinny noise of a television. It was the first sign of life I'd seen since I left the temporary HQ down at the marina.

The stone steps up to the porch were slick with ice, so I went up slowly and carefully. I stopped in front of the door and listened. It's good practice to pause before knocking on a strange door, just in case someone is lurking on the other side with a loaded firearm. I heard nothing, so I rang the bell and waited.

Still nothing.

I pulled out my phone and checked for bars – also nothing.

I checked the nearest window. The curtains were open and I put my face close to the cold glass. Inside, I could make out the shadowy shapes of a beige couch, a pine end table and the dully reflective rectangle of a wall-mounted television. At the rear, a door was open into a hallway leading back into the house. I caught a sense of random movement among the shadows, like wind catching at curtains and flurries of snow.

I fumbled my flashlight out of the pocket of my parka

and lit up the interior. There were the remains of a coffee table in front of the couch. The glass top was now a spray of glittering crystal across the carpet. A coffee cup lay on its side among the debris. There was no other obvious damage in the room, so it could have been an accident rather than signs of a struggle, but I didn't like it. Especially when I angled my flashlight into the hallway and saw that the back door was hanging open.

I worked my way around the house and into the unfenced backyard. There were tracks in the snow leading from the open door and out the left side of the yard – heading down the slope toward the house with the light on. I approached the door, careful to avoid disturbing the tracks, and crouched down for a closer look.

Fresh snow had softened the contours, but the drift outside the door had been trampled almost down to the level of the patio. I couldn't make out individual tracks but it looked like dozens of people had come and gone. Something I couldn't identify had made strange misshapen holes and gashes either side of the trail.

And there were streaks of green and red along the trail that glistened in the beam of my flashlight.

Despite the cold, I unzipped my parka enough to draw my firearm and then, holding it close to my chest, I gingerly climbed the back steps and entered the house.

3

There was a smell inside the hallway. Woodsmoke tinged with coffee grounds. Snow had drifted over the threshold to gather on the floor, and the walls were cold to the touch. The back door must have been open for a good while.

'Mr. Henderson,' I called. 'Are you home?'

I listened for a ten count and tried again.

'This is the FBI – is there anyone in the house?'

I could hear my pulse in my ears and the wind picking up outside.

There was a light switch just inside the door – I flipped it and was mildly surprised when the lights came on. I closed the back door behind me and looked around. There was a kitchen through an open door to the right, the stovetop and the counters tidy and clean. To the left was a room with bookshelves and a desk. I put the light on in there, but I didn't linger.

The first sweep through a target house is all about threats and agent safety. Investigation comes after you know some bad guy isn't going to spring out of a closet with a shotgun.

Ideally, of course, you're not supposed to do it on your own.

The living room was much as I'd seen through the window, although with the lights on I could see where broken glass from the coffee table had been ground into the dove-grey carpet in a trail toward the doorway I was standing in. Something brown and glistening had been spilled on the carpet and then smeared into streaks pointing in the same direction. I glanced back down the hall and spotted traces of the same stuff where the baseboard met the bare floorboards.

The ground coffee and woodsmoke smell was stronger in the living room, but I was beginning to suspect that these were not real odours but *vestigia*. In which case, something supernatural had happened in the room – possibly to Patrick Henderson.

I stepped into the front hall and, leaving the light off, I went up the staircase as fast and as quietly as I could. The *vestigia* faded as I reached the landing. The king-size in the master bedroom was unmade and the room had the stale winter aroma of resident male. What I guessed was a guest bedroom was half-filled with storage boxes, and there were traces of shaving foam and bristles in the sink in the bathroom. I left the lights on in every room and made my way back down to the lounge.

I pulled on my gloves and squatted down to have a look at the mysterious stains. It wasn't blood – I know what blood looks like. But it did glisten like the slime trail left by slugs and snails. I hadn't brought an evidence kit with me, and the nearest professional evidence team was probably at the Bayfield County Sheriff's headquarters in Washburn. Ten miles and one blocked highway to the south.

There was an old-fashioned push-button phone on a side table in the hall. On the off chance, I dialled *69 on the landline in the study and made a note of the local number it returned. I took the call-back option and was passed on to a voicemail service.

'Eloise Public Library,' said a woman's voice, and proceeded to give instructions on how to reserve and return books and how to pay overdue fines. 'Because I know your conscience will not let you sleep until you do.' Followed by a theatrical cackle.

Then I used the same phone to call the Wausau field office, who patched me through to Special Agent Sean Doughty.

'You think he's been abducted?' he asked after I detailed the scene.

I said that's what it looked like, and he promised to rustle up an evidence team just as soon as the pass could be cleared.

'Failing that,' he said, 'I'll see if I can arrange a helicopter.'

I said I'd appreciate that and he told me to take care.

I used my useless cell phone to take pictures of the lounge and the trail down the hall, and then went to search the study.

There was a plain but antique walnut desk supporting a tower PC, a pen jar and an old-fashioned two-level wire-frame in and out tray. I turned on the PC; the fan whirred, but instead of booting up I got the blue screen of death. It didn't even have an error message, just multiple columns of incomprehensible hexadecimal. I turned it off and left it for the promised evidence team.

The top desk drawer contained a box of pens, a chequebook with only a few cheques missing, two errant rubber bands and a packet of tacks. The bottom drawer was larger, and held stationery including a yellow legal pad. I slanted the pad toward the light but there were no indentations on the top page.

No day planner or notebook, which was odd for Henderson's generation, and no sign of a cell phone, although a charge cable was plugged into the wall socket beside the desk. There were two waist-high bookcases either side of the window. The bottom shelves held box files hand-lettered with years – going back to 1998. I picked the latest and opened it, and found it filled with familiar reams of invoices, bills and official looking letters. His tax accounts, at a guess.

The upper shelves held a collection of thrillers, local history and fishing guides. A couple of occult books caught my eye, and among them an antique hardback whose spine was half hanging off. I opened it to the title page, which read: *Identifying the Unusual* by Ida May Machon. The publisher was listed as Important Books Ltd, New York, 1946. I opened on a page at random and read:

Here we turn to the manifestations that can be created by a confluence of natural forces, or by human agency. The practitioners of the Old World call such things genii locorum, *but here we are mostly concerned with those manifestations known as malignancies.*

'Practitioners', '*genii locorum*' and 'malignancies' were

all key words that indicated that this was a book about real magic, probably written by a practitioner herself. I flicked through the rest of the book and found references to *formae*, *fey*, Thomas Jefferson and Sir Isaac Newton, which confirmed it.

A flash of yellow drew me to a page near the end of the book. It was a sticky page marker that had obviously come unstuck and migrated across the page and into the spine. I scanned the pages it was stuck between, and they mainly related to legends of human sacrifice among the native population of Canada. Ida May Machon gave little credence to reports of spirits being summoned up to attack farmers in Quebec.

The French have always been prone to exaggeration in these matters, she wrote.

My evidence kit was in my closet back in Manassas. I'd been relying on Agent Doughty bringing his up from Wausau, so I was going to have to improvise. I rooted around in the stationery in the desk drawer and found a padded envelope. I labelled it with a Sharpie and slipped the book inside. I'd been amassing quite a collection of genuinely magical titles in a special restricted section at the FBI Library in Quantico, and some day I'll have to take time off to catalogue them. I left it on the desk where I wouldn't forget it.

There was a gun safe mounted on the wall by the door. As befitted a former agent, this was a solid metal affair securely fastened to floor and wall and locked with a digital keypad. I knew better than to randomly enter numbers, and so I left that for the evidence team as well.

Then I stepped out the back door and started following the trail down the hill.

'Go away!' shouted a voice from inside the house.

Henderson's neighbours lived in a smaller one-storey shingle house on a lot that appeared to have been graded in anticipation of a much larger dwelling. Night had started drawing in while I'd conducted my search, but the weather was clearing, the clouds running west away from the lake to reveal a sky of glittering blackness. The wind had picked up at ground level, too, but despite the chill I kept my parka partially unzipped in case I needed to draw my pistol in a hurry.

The trail through the snow had run diagonally downslope, through the snow piled by ploughs in the gutter, before vanishing into the salted slush that covered the road surface. Whatever had happened had happened before the snowploughs had gone through. Once I found out when that was, I would have a time frame for the abduction.

I was sure it *was* an abduction because something person-sized had been dragged through the snow. Assuming they kept going in a straight line, they'd have crossed the road diagonally in front of the neighbours' house.

'My name is Special Agent Kimberley Reynolds,' I called, and shifted sideways so that I was no longer standing directly in front of the door. 'From the FBI. Could you come to the door, please?'

'What do you want?'

The voice was just behind the door – a woman, I

thought – with a fragile edge that suggested age. The age might explain her caution, although these small towns usually carry at least the illusion of safety.

'I'm looking for Patrick Henderson,' I said.

'He lives next door,' said the woman.

My cheeks and nose were starting to go numb, and a cold wind was blowing into the unzipped front of my parka.

'He's not at home,' I said, keeping the impatience out of my voice.

'They took him,' said the voice.

'Who took him?' I asked, and reflexively turned to put the door jamb at my back and scan the road to left and right. There was a long pause, but in the stillness I could hear someone breathing on the other side of the door.

They took him.

Either the owner of the voice had witnessed the abduction, or Henderson was with her and she was covering for him. Or she was being held under duress and being told to get rid of me.

I had to gain access, if only to ensure it wasn't the latter.

'Could you let me in, please?' I said. 'I need to ask you some questions about the abduction.'

'What abduction?'

'The one you say you witnessed.'

There was a pause, and then she let me in, but only after making me hold my ID up to the door's peephole first. After that, locks rattled, the door opened and I found myself face to face with a short, dumpy senior

31

citizen with blue eyes, a long aquiline nose and thick white hair hanging loose to her shoulders. She was wearing a blue and green quilted housecoat, thick blue tights, pink furry boot slippers, and was holding an illegally shortened Remington 870 far too casually in the crook of her arm.

I couldn't fault her weapon choice, though. For home defence you really can't beat a sawn-off pump-action shotgun. Maximum deterrence with minimal risk of collateral.

I suggested that she secure her weapon, and she stowed it in a glass-fronted walnut cabinet beside the fireplace. With that danger removed, I unzipped my parka and looked around. For a dwelling that was only marginally larger than your average trailer, the interior seemed remarkably spacious. The woman, who introduced herself as Mrs Rhonda Macklewright, had obvious taste. I could see it in the way the covers on the couch harmonised with the floor rugs.

Once she had safely disarmed herself, Rhonda offered me a coffee, which I gratefully accepted, and asked whether I might use her bathroom. I was shown to a small room at the back of the house with a stone floor and an old-fashioned claw-footed white enamel tub with no shower fittings. After I'd washed my hands, I took the opportunity to check the one bedroom and a second smaller room that served as storage. Satisfied that nobody else was hiding in the house, I returned to the living room, where I was handed a pot-brewed coffee in a white mug with ELOISE ICE ROAD printed on it in pale blue letters.

'How well do you know Mr. Henderson?' I asked as Rhonda settled herself opposite me in a paisley patterned armchair that matched the couch I was sitting on.

'Is Patrick in trouble?' she asked. There was a forced brightness in her voice.

'He isn't at home,' I said. 'I'm worried that something may have happened to him.'

'Have you tried the Old Pub?' she said. 'It's on Main Street. That's where he is most nights.'

Her eyes flicked away from me, looking at the wall, the TV, the window. In a formal interview I'd have suspected she was deliberately lying, but instead she was coming across as fearful. What did she know that she didn't want to talk about?

'It's still the afternoon,' I said.

Mrs Macklewright blinked and touched her housecoat as if realising for the first time she was wearing it.

'So it is,' she said. 'In that case, you might try the library. He's been spending a lot of time there since we got our new librarian.'

'Really?'

'Name of Miss Sadie Clarkson,' said Mrs Macklewright, putting stress on the 'Miss'. 'Came up all the way from New Orleans, would you believe. Said she got tired of the humidity.'

The library again.

'You said someone took him,' I said.

'Did I?' said Mrs Macklewright, but her eyes flicked away to the right and then down to contemplate her coffee.

'You did,' I said. 'I said he wasn't at his house and you said, "They took him."'

Mrs Macklewright turned to gaze at her TV, which was showing a frozen frame of what I recognised as *The Golden Girls*, Blanche and Rose looking slightly squashed because of the widescreen ratio.

'Who were "they"?' I asked.

Mrs Macklewright turned back to me and gave an apologetic smile.

'I think it was a dream,' she said. 'The kind you have when you're waking up. I dreamed I heard footsteps and dragging sounds and Patrick cursing.' She shrugged. 'But when I looked outside there was nothing to see.'

It took some gentle questioning to tease out the details. Mrs Macklewright had been in her bed, dozing, when she had the dream. She said that in the winter she didn't leave her bed – 'except for necessities' – until the sun came up.

'I make myself a thermos of coffee before I go to bed,' she said.

She liked to read in bed in the morning because these days she drifted off too quickly at the end of the day. This morning, despite the book being the latest Jodi Picoult, she must have nodded off, because she had one of those disturbing dreams.

'The ones when you dream you are awake in your own bed,' she said. 'And you don't know you're dreaming.'

It had been still dark and not yet seven o'clock. Mrs Macklewright had dreamed that she had been woken up by shouting outside her window. She had climbed out of bed, shivering in the cold, and looked out. Her bedroom window looked north up the slope to Patrick Henderson's house, and it was his shouting that had awoken her.

His shouts grew louder, and she saw him silhouetted against the streetlights, being dragged along toward the street.

'He definitely didn't want to go,' she said.

'Did you see who was dragging him?' I asked.

'That's how I know it was a dream,' said Mrs Macklewright.

Or rather a nightmare, because the figures that dragged her neighbour away weren't people exactly.

'I saw antlers and muzzles,' she said. 'Or thought I did. They were shambling like they were drunk, or not really the right shape. I tried to go get my gun but I couldn't make myself move. That's when I realised it was a dream and got back into bed.'

She had glanced at her alarm clock before pulling the covers up over her head.

'It was 7:30,' she said.

About the time I was checking in at Dulles.

4

The sky was clear when I stepped out of Mrs Macklewright's house, and the temperature had noticeably dropped. I pulled my scarf up over my nose while I considered my next move.

Whatever had happened to Patrick Henderson had happened before dawn that morning. Mrs Macklewright had experienced her dream at 07:30, and the drag marks had been obliterated by the town plough that had passed through, according to Mrs Macklewright, sometime between eight and nine.

But what *had* happened to Patrick Henderson?

I crunched through the snow and studied the place where the drag marks reached the sidewalk and the dirty snow had been piled up by the recent ploughing. A day's worth of snow had blurred the outline of the tracks and I couldn't discern any individual footprints. Nor did I sense any *vestigia*, although being largely self-taught I couldn't be certain I hadn't overlooked them.

But I could be certain that I was definitely dealing with a case with 'unusual characteristics'. Mrs Macklewright had seen something so outlandish that she couldn't reconcile it with her own view of normality. This is not unusual with eyewitnesses who are exposed to sudden trauma or the horrific aftermaths of gun or bomb attacks, and it goes doubly so for those who are exposed to the supernatural. The mind rationalises the inexplicable – we didn't see what we thought we saw or, as with Mrs Macklewright, it was an hallucination or a dream.

Patrick Henderson had been dragged off by somebody – or something – that was beyond normal experience. And this had occurred less than a week after he contacted the Bureau. Just before he was taken, an ice tornado roared in from the lake and flattened the town hall, and freak blizzards cut Eloise off from the outside world.

I didn't think any of this was a coincidence.

The Bureau expects its agents to own their cases. You may work as part of an FBI team or multi-agency task force, but the agent in charge is expected to get the job done with what they have on hand.

I had myself, a rental and a clear set of tracks.

The ploughed road had frozen over with a treacherous film of ice, so I trod carefully until I was safely on the sidewalk opposite where the tracks ended. Then I used my flashlight to trace their path down the hill and then their path across the road, assuming they'd kept on in a straight line. Ten feet down from where I stood, I could see the snow was disturbed and something glistened in the beam of my flashlight.

The lots on this side of the street had seemingly never been graded, let alone occupied. Instead, they sloped upward to a ridge and were still dotted with fir and beech trees. Where the sidewalk met the slope there was a trampled area three feet across. And partially hidden among undergrowth was the decapitated head of a deer.

I squatted down for a closer look. It was the head of a large adult buck. He still had his antlers, which were a good size. When I brushed away the snow, I found that the neck ended in ragged flaps of skin, muscle and viscera. An impossible length of spine extended nakedly out from the neck. I grew up hunting and I'd never seen an injury like that on a wild animal before.

I pulled off one glove and used my phone to take pictures. There wasn't much blood visible, just a few splashes around the neck. Some of it was probably buried under fresh snow, but certainly not as much as I would have expected from such a terrible wound.

I saw antlers and muzzles, Mrs Macklewright had said.

Had the buck's head been a trophy carried along by whoever had abducted Henderson? Perhaps dumped when carrying it became too onerous. If this was what convinced Mrs Macklewright she was dreaming, was it possible that his kidnappers had been mundane, ordinary flesh-and-blood people?

God, I hope so.

The disturbance continued up the slope on the same diagonal track as before. I saw broken branches among the undergrowth, and a birch sapling that had been broken at shoulder height and pushed aside. Under the trees, less snow had fallen and the actual tracks were easier to see, although I couldn't make out any distinct boot prints.

I followed it up, keeping to the left as much as possible to preserve the tracks. Probably futile, but it's best not to destroy evidence unless you have to. I was less than twenty feet from the ridgeline when I heard movement above. I unzipped my parka again and pulled off my right glove. The cold bit my fingers and I stuffed my hand inside so that it rested on the grip of my Glock 22. It was awkward, but then so is a bullet in the face.

I heard the noise again. A rhythmic crunching, like giant footsteps. Close enough that I could pinpoint its direction – straight up the line of the tracks I was following. I pulled my gun, It felt heavy and warm in my hand. I widened my stance. Then I shone my flashlight up toward the noise.

Through the undergrowth I caught a flash of something man-sized and reflective orange.

'Is that you, Agent Reynolds?' called a voice I recognised – William Boyd.

'Is that you, Mr. Boyd?' I called back.

'Yes,' he said. 'I was wondering where you'd got to. Are you coming up or do you want me to come down?'

'You'd better come down,' I said. 'Slowly.'

The rhythmic crunching restarted and a figure in a familiar bulky parka and reflective vest stepped into the beam of my flashlight. The hood was still up and a scarf obscured the face. He was wearing a pair of snowshoes that crunched on the snow with every step. He stopped ten feet away and put up his hand to block the light from his eyes.

'Hello?' he said.

'Can you lower your scarf, sir?' I said.

'OK,' he said and, moving with exaggerated slowness, pulled the cloth down to reveal his face. I approached for a closer look. It was definitely William Boyd.

40

I thanked him and gratefully holstered my gun.

I told him to stay where he was and climbed up the slope to join him. As I'd feared, his snowshoes had effectively obliterated the tracks I'd been following, although I could still make out the general direction they'd gone from the broken branches among the undergrowth.

I handed Boyd my flashlight so I could put my right glove back on before my fingers froze off.

'Did you follow a track down to here?' I asked.

'Yes,' said Boyd. 'Were you following it the other way?'

'Yes,' I said, and flexed my fingers as pins and needles shot through them. 'Where does it lead?'

'I think you're going to want to see this for yourself,' he said.

So I followed Boyd up the slope, finding it easier going stepping in his outsized footprints. The trees and undergrowth gave way at the crest of the ridge and I stopped with Boyd to look out over the town.

There was no moon in the freezing sky, but the town's power was obviously still running because the downtown grid was still illuminated by its streetlights. The lake was a sheet of starless darkness stretching beyond the lights of the marina.

Between the ridge and lake was a patch of brighter lights. Floods, I realised, lighting what was left of a house that had been demolished down to its foundations. There were tiny figures in hard hats picking their way through the rubble. A yellow backhoe started up with a roar of diesel and started pawing at the ground.

'Your ice tornado?' I asked.

'What?'

I leaned closer and pulled down my scarf; he followed suit.

'Was that caused by your ice tornado?'

'Yes,' said Boyd. 'It came ashore in front of the town hall, and drove inland.'

He pointed, and I followed his finger to where the shattered remains of a yacht were picked out by street-lamps by the marina. I recognised the splayed-out wreckage of the town hall and the large barn-like build-ing that served as the emergency response centre.

You could trace the tornado's course by the irregular patches of darkness where it had demolished houses and overthrown streetlamps.

'Any casualties?' I asked.

'They're just checking the last house, but it seems not,' said Boyd.

He said something else but I missed it because I'd just realised that the path of destruction lined up per-fectly with where we were standing on the ridge.

'What was that?'

'I said it was a bit of a miracle, really,' said Boyd. 'That no one was seriously injured.'

'How did you find me?'

'I wasn't looking for you in particular,' he said. 'I was following the destruction track.'

'So it led you up here.'

'It appears to have lost energy rapidly after it came ashore,' said Boyd. 'By the time it got up here it can't have been much more than a whirlwind. I'm surprised it made it this far.'

I felt a chill in the pit of my stomach. Connecting

Henderson's possible abduction to something as violently destructive as the ice tornado implied more power than I wanted to think about.

'You said ice tornadoes were rare,' I said. 'How rare?'

'We have a few reliable accounts,' said Boyd. 'But all of them report a snow funnel forming inside an existing thunderstorm. This one came ashore among a conventional snow storm with no supercell – which is unprecedented.'

Did somebody come ashore under cover of this unprecedented tornado? Did they grab Patrick Henderson and then retreat the way they'd arrived? Had these unknown somebodies created the tornado *as* cover for the snatch? When I was a kid, an F3 hit my home town. I was sheltering in our storm shelter and you could feel the power of it through the concrete floor.

So far my encounters with the supernatural had been low-key and largely ambiguous. Even my experiences in London had been confined to mysterious lights and people who could rip chunks out of concrete with their bare hands. But I'd been warned that magic could manifest itself on a grand scale . . . although I'd been thinking cracks in the asphalt, not major weather events.

Had Henderson seen this coming?

Probably not, or he'd have been duty-bound to warn the Bureau in that first call, even if only in general terms. But he must have suspected something.

I asked Boyd if he knew where the town library was, and he pointed out Allouez Avenue.

'Follow that west and it's on the corner with 6th Street,' he said. 'If you're going now I'll meet you there.'

I asked what he wanted with the library.

'Newspaper archive,' he said. 'I want to look at the weather reports.'

5

With the sidewalk icy in the freezing stillness, it was easier to walk up the snow-covered kerb strip. This was still hard work, though, and I was sweating by the time I reached Patrick Henderson's house. I went in the unlocked back door, retrieved the magic book I'd left in the home office and left via the front to climb back into the Toyota. It started first time, and I let the engine run for a couple of minutes while the heater fought to raise the temperature above freezing. Once I could reliably handle the steering wheel without risking frostbite, I put the Toyota in drive and made my way slowly and carefully down the hill. I took the next right on to Allouez Avenue. The town fathers of Eloise had really committed to the idea of a road grid that ran east–west and north–south, and they weren't going to let anything pesky like geography get in their way. As a result, once you were away from the lakeside, no street in Eloise was flat and level. Allouez Avenue was no exception, and climbed steeply enough to make my wheels spin if I stepped too hard on the gas.

The town library was a nondescript modern brick-built affair with a flat roof. It stood on the corner where the intersection with 6th Street made a mercifully flat stretch that allowed me to park without worrying about the efficiency of the Toyota's handbrake. A pickup truck was also parked outside. I got out and gave it a once-over. It was a Ford Raptor in fire-engine red. If the lack of snow hadn't given it away, then the badger bumper sticker and the *Meteorologists Do It in the Rain* decal in the rear window would have identified it as Boyd's. Equipment canisters were secured under a tarp in the flatbed, and it had a roof-mounted snorkel, an amber lightbar and studded tyres. Mr. Boyd obviously took his all-weather transport seriously.

If the weather got worse, I wondered if I might have to commandeer it.

I kept a grip on the freezing metal railing as I walked up the concrete steps to the entrance. The windows were all lit up and through them I could see shelves of books and fluorescent lights hanging overhead.

Mama was always suspicious of my home town's library. She used to complain that it was too big, too ugly and too full of literature. Not that my mama was against reading, you understand, but that she was worried that the presence of so many books might distract folks from the one book that really mattered.

That library was not what you'd call pretty, being made of rough concrete in the same style as the Puzzle Palace in DC. But inside it was bright, cheerful, full of books and, more importantly for teenaged me, full of quiet nooks for study and liaisons with Ryan Poulson.

Mama did not approve of Ryan because he was two years older than me and a Catholic. She also suspected him of dealing drugs, which was no more true of Ryan than it was of any other high school senior. To me, his appeal was that he had a car, a sense of humour and a plan to get out of Enid as soon as he graduated. Ironically, these days he runs a medical marijuana business in Los Angeles. I have neglected to inform my mama of this fact.

Heat engulfed me as I pushed open the front doors and into a small atrium. There was a glass-fronted notice board on the left and a cork board for cards and messages on the right. Sweat started prickling my armpits, and I took a moment to pull off my gloves and parka before stepping through the inner doors.

The library was all one room and had to take up almost all of the building. A horseshoe counter sat in the middle of an open space in the centre, surrounded by reading tables. In the far right corner, shelves enclosed a patch of yellow and orange painted floor strewn with child-sized soft furniture in matching colours. In the far left I could see reading desks and microfiche readers through gaps in the shelves. A black-haired man in a red long-sleeved T-shirt sat hunched in front of one – I glimpsed enough profile to identify William Boyd. A dark woman with black eyes emerged from behind a stack and spotted me.

'Are you Special Agent Kimberley Reynolds?'

She had an educated Southern accent and I guessed that this was Sadie Clarkson, town librarian, up from New Orleans. She was a small, narrow-shouldered, middle-aged woman bulked out by a thick wool cardigan worn over an equally thick sweater in complementary shades of russet and dark red. Below this she wore black ski pants tucked into white and red chequered knitted slipper boots.

I introduced myself, confirmed her identity and shook her hand. Her fingers were slender and cold but her grip was firm.

'How can I help you?' she asked, and I asked if she knew Patrick Henderson.

'Sure,' she said. 'Has something happened to him?'

'Why do you ask?'

She hesitated.

'He left a couple of funny messages last night,' said Sadie. 'And now you're here.'

I knew his last call from his landline had been to the library, but it's always best not to make assumptions so I asked what form the messages had taken. Sadie confirmed that he'd left them on the library's voicemail.

'He didn't call you direct?' I asked.

'He didn't have my cell number,' said Sadie. 'I don't give it out as a rule.'

I asked whether she'd kept the voice messages, and Sadie took me over to the counter and pulled the library phone out from its niche and put it in front of me. She hadn't bothered to establish a security code for the voicemail.

'I'd only forget it,' she said, and stabbed the star code into the keypad and handed me the handset.

A computer voice gave the time of the message as 19:23 the previous evening.

'Sadie,' said a voice I recognised, from the FBI's switchboard recording, as Patrick Henderson's. 'Has anyone been asking after the journal? If they do, stall

48

them and let me know. Shit, you've gone home.'

There was a beep and a second message timed at just under an hour later, at 20:17.

'Hi, Sadie. Whatever you do, don't give the journal to anybody else. In fact, if anyone asks, deny you have it.'

The incoming number matched Patrick Henderson's landline both times. I'd called him earlier that day and not got through – obviously local calls had been unaffected by the snow.

I looked at Sadie, who was shaking her head.

'I should have known something was wrong,' she said, and looked quickly around the library as if checking for intruders. 'What do you think might have happened?'

'What's this journal he's talking about?'

'Sorry,' said Sadie. 'What was that?'

'The journal Henderson mentions,' I said. 'Do you know what it is?'

There was a hesitation of the kind that's familiar to law officers, schoolteachers and mothers. The one that marks somebody thinking quickly as to whether they can get away with a lie or not.

'It's in the back,' she said.

Sadie led me back to her combination office, staff kitchen and storeroom. As we passed the microfiche machines, Boyd turned and raised his hand in greeting. I nodded back and he turned back to the machine. There was a clank and a whirr and the front page of a newspaper came into focus.

Sadie unlocked one of two vintage filing cabinets, opened the bottom drawer and pulled out a rectangular red enamel cookie tin. Placing the tin on her desk, she opened it up to reveal an oblong wrapped in pink tissue paper.

'We need to wash our hands before we handle it,' said Sadie. 'And wear these.'

She handed me a pair of clean cotton gloves.

We took turns at the kitchen sink and Sadie took the opportunity to put a kettle on the burner and offered me coffee. When I said yes, she stuck her head out around the door and asked if Boyd wanted one, too.

While she measured coffee into the press, I carefully dried my hands, donned the gloves and unwrapped the package. It was a journal, approximately eleven by five inches. The leather-bound cover was scuffed and discoloured in places. When I bent down to look closer at it, I caught a trace of a distinctive smell. Musty, with a hint of mildew.

'I came across it when I was clearing out the cupboards,' said Sadie, as I gingerly opened the journal and turned to its first page. The writing was small, cramped and so smudged by water that it was impossible to read.

'The bit Patrick was interested in starts two-thirds in,' said Sadie. 'There's a bookmark.'

Which turned out to be a sterile balsa wood tongue depressor. There were several more marking places further on in the journal. Sadie stood behind me and urged me to handle the book carefully.

'Do you know whose journal this is?' I asked.

'Patrick believed it was written by one Ephraim Wright of Poughkeepsie, New York,' said Sadie. 'Part of the infamous disappearing expedition of 1843.'

I wondered if this was Cymbeline's lost expedition. I

asked who had recovered the journal in the first place.

'I did,' said Sadie. 'Found it in that cookie tin with a mess of buttons. I was "cataloguing"' – she made air quotes around the word – 'the storeroom. They're opening a library up at Red Cliffs and they asked me to check for local history materials. These things can get lost for decades. Especially if they relate to Native history.'

Talking shop had obviously calmed Sadie down but I could still sense an undercurrent of disquiet – possibly even fear – behind her chatter.

I opened the page to the first tongue depressor and found that, although smudged and blurred in places, the penmanship was well-formed and clear. Without the start of the narrative, I had to infer the context. Still, Ephraim Wright was such a prolific complainer that certain things became clear. He would much rather have left America's manifest destiny to others, since, as he acidly put it, *They appeared to derive much enjoyment from the privations of the territory.* He had particular scorn for Captain William Marsh, whom he often referred to as *that goddamned Virginian,* and whom he blamed for trapping them in the winter camp when the lake froze over in January 1844. From this and other hints, I could confirm that Marsh had been leading an expedition by the Virginia Gentlemen's Company. Probably the one that Cymbeline had mentioned. Especially when Wright bitterly opined that he thought that the local Natives were *devils enough* without searching for something even more godless. Despite his carping, it was clear that the expedition had only survived with the help of the local Native Americans, who traded with them for supplies. In late January the camp was visited by *a handsome Indian brave of no more than twelve years* who claimed to know the whereabouts of the *abomination*.

I checked back over the pages as far as I could, but it seemed this was the first specific mention of the *abomination*. Although Wright had alluded to Captain Marsh's obsession with something, it was never clearly defined. I got the distinct impression that hunting this *abomination* was the primary objective of the expedition.

Word of this created great excitement among the company from Virginia, and in particular, in the breast of our gallant Captain. When the young brave offered to guide us across the ice to the abomination's lair, Marsh, fearing the ice would not last, threatened to set out at once.

Ephraim immediately volunteered to stay behind to keep the camp and tend to the several members of the expedition who had fallen, or at least claimed to have fallen, ill.

There is no doubt in my mind that I might have remonstrated harder against this dire action, but I am equally convinced that Captain Marsh would have paid me no heed. He saw himself as a superior gentleman and a scholar and valued my opinion not at all.

The morning that Marsh and the bulk of the expedition set out to cross the ice, Marsh's chief lieutenant, Oliver

Southwell, took Ephraim aside and presented him with a letter.

He bade me to deliver this letter to his wife should things go awry, as he feared they would. I watched him join Marsh and the perfidious Indian at the head of the company as they set out in the early morn.

Never to return. I skimmed the rest of the journal, but it mainly concerned Ephraim and his remaining companions waiting out the winter and then returning to Sault Sainte Marie once the lake had thawed.

I carefully rewrapped the journal and replaced it in the cookie tin.

Patrick Henderson had warned Sadie not to give the journal to anyone else, to deny its existence if asked. Sadie had given it up to me without a qualm, or even asking to see my badge. Because she had been expecting me, or because she hadn't taken Patrick seriously?

Or perhaps she felt that, with Patrick Henderson missing, circumstances had changed. Had I told her he was missing? I couldn't remember, which was sloppy on my part. I'd have to watch my step.

I realised that Sadie had left the staff room/office but not before leaving a cup of coffee beside me on the desk – it was now lukewarm. I felt a sudden troubling dislocation; how long had I spent reading the journal? I checked my watch – it was only just turning six. Less than twenty minutes.

I got up and looked out the door.

Boyd was still at the microfiche machine, but turned away to look up at Sadie, who was perched on the adjacent desk, red and white knitted slipper socks kicking back and forth. They were talking too softly for me to overhear, and I got the strong impression they knew each other fairly well. I'd have to establish what Boyd's connection with the librarian and the locality was.

I picked up the cookie can and walked over to join them.

'I'm going to have to take this as evidence,' I said.

Sadie propelled herself off the table like a teenager and squared up to me.

'Evidence for what?' she said.

'I'm not at liberty to say,' I said.

'You never said what had happened to Patrick,' she said.

'He's gone missing.'

'What's that got to do with the FBI?'

'Good question,' said Boyd, swinging his chair around to face me.

'He used to work for the Bureau,' I said.

'I know,' said Sadie. 'He used to talk about it.'

Given that Patrick Henderson's records had proved hard to come by, I was about to ask exactly what he'd talked about, when the phone rang.

I kept my eye on Boyd as Sadie walked back to the office to answer it. He smiled. It was a good smile, but I'm trained not to be distracted by such things.

'You can't take that,' he said, nodding at the cookie tin. 'That's a vital piece of Native history.'

'So you've read it?'

'Of course,' he said. 'Although I was really reading it for the weather reports.'

'When was that?'

But before Boyd could answer, Sadie called my name from the office.

'Agent Reynolds,' she said, 'the police chief would like a word.'

6

The police chiefs of small towns, in my experience, need to have good social skills. Keeping the peace in small communities is often more about brokering compromises rather than strictly enforcing the law. Back at Quantico, wonder PA Jan had looked this one up while I was in the air this morning, and emailed me their findings after I'd landed. His name was Cameron Santire. He'd served as a Marine in Afghanistan and Iraq before joining the Madison PD, where he served three years before being recruited to run Eloise's four-strong police department.

'I need to ask you a favour,' he said once I'd identified myself. 'We've had a call from a hotel up the shore. They've reported a disturbance on their grounds. We're a little tied up at the moment and I wondered if you might see your way to checking it out.'

'What kind of disturbance?'

'A possible 10-76– certainly someone tried to break in,' he said. 'The fella that made the report was from the BIA, so I figured it might have a federal angle.'

As an excuse to rope me in, it was pretty thin, although technically the Bureau of Indian Affairs and the FBI did have some jurisdiction in what was still quaintly called Indian Territory. Still, I'd heard rumours that the BIA had its own secretive section that dealt with unusual characteristics, so they might be worth talking to. Certainly I was at a loss how to proceed until the roads cleared and my backup arrived.

As my mama frequently said if she caught me with time on my hands, *there's no point lollygagging – there's always something that needs to be done.*

I told the chief that I'd see if I could get over and attend the scene.

'Sadie will give you directions,' he said, sounding relieved.

He gave me the name of the hotel, the Eloise Lakeview Lodge, and the BIA guy, Scott Walker. He also warned me that the weather was closing in again and there was a good chance the power would go down. After the call I went to the nearest window and pressed my face to the cold glass. It was snowing heavily – big fat flakes.

Boyd joined me at the window.

'Stellar dendrites,' he said. 'Another front is coming in from the lake.'

'Is it going to get worse?' I asked.

'I haven't seen the latest imaging,' he said. 'But I'd say probably a couple of hours of this. Unless we get another tornado.'

I thought of my rented Toyota and how it had laboured up the hill.

'Can you give me a ride to this hotel?' I asked.

'OK,' he said. 'I need to check a weather station near there anyway.'

'That's convenient,' I said.

'It is, isn't it?'

'Let's talk about my journal first,' said Sadie, coming up behind us.

While Boyd warmed up his truck and cleaned off his windshield, I took the opportunity to transfer my spare magazine, dry socks and my emergency Tampax to the pockets of my parka. I took the magic book back up to the library and asked Sadie to keep it safe with the journal. I watched as she checked the title page, but there was no sign she recognised its significance. Leaving the journal with her had helped mollify her, and at least she was coming around to the idea it was evidence. And I figured a library was as safe a place as any to leave both books until I got back.

'How much material about the Marsh expedition do you have?' I asked.

She narrowed her eyes and I could see she was considering not answering just to spite me. Then she shrugged.

'Primary material?' she said. 'Nothing else. There could be secondary references in the newspaper archive. You might want to ask down at the Lakeview Lodge – they make a big thing out of local heritage. Brings in the tourists.'

I carefully made my way back down the steps to where Boyd's truck was gently steaming and climbed up into the passenger seat. We belted up and I waited until he'd negotiated the steep slope down toward the lake before asking him whether he was from Eloise originally.

'What makes you think I'm from here?'

'You seem very friendly with the locals,' I said.

'Sadie isn't a local,' he said. 'She's only been here less than a year.'

'Deputy Larson?'

'Patricia? She's from Ashland, although she did go to high school in Bayfield.'

'Very friendly,' I said.

'You got me,' he said. 'I'm from Fitchburg, but my parents were from Bayfield. Got a bus load of relatives spread all over the peninsula.'

'Red Cliff as well?'

'Is this you trying to ask me whether I'm an Indian?' said Boyd.

Unbelievably, I actually blushed – fortunately Boyd was too busy concentrating on the road to notice.

'I guess so,' I said. 'Are you?'

'Red Cliff Band Ojibwe,' he said. 'Can sing the song, dance the dance and cook the frybread.'

'Is the frybread important?' I asked.

He laughed.

'You've never worked Indian Country before, have you?'

I said I hadn't.

'Then maybe later I'll give you a chance to find out,' he said.

The houses petered out on either side and a hill rose sharply on the right, steep tree-covered slopes, the dark vertical lines of the trunks vanishing into the dirty white haze of the low-hanging cloud.

'Eloise Point,' said Boyd. 'The weather station's at the top. I'll drop you off at the hotel and then head up.'

I said I'd rather he waited for me to assess the risk before vanishing up the hill, and he agreed.

'If you're quick, you could come up with me,' he said. 'The view might be spectacular.'

'Might be?'

'Or possibly just a couple of yards,' he said. 'It depends on the height of the clouds.'

We turned off the highway on to a private lane that curved downslope toward the shore. Oaks lined the lane, bare limbs reaching overhead to form a winding processional that opened up on to a snow-covered lawn. There were muffled lumps and bumps that hinted at an ornamental garden.

A long white single-storey building loomed out of the snow. It had a steep shingled roof and a yellow trimmed veranda that ran its entire length. Electric carriage lamps cast warm pools of light over benches and love seats that had been swaddled in tarps for the winter. There was a Cherokee and an old Ford pickup parked in front of the main doors. The Ford was half-buried in snow, but the Cherokee had arrived recently enough for me to see the Department of the Interior, Bureau of Indian Affairs seal on the door. It needed retouching, because a long scrape disfigured the central image of an eagle standing on a red, white and blue shield.

Boyd pulled up as close to the main entrance as he could, and we dashed across in the cutting wind, up the stairs and pushed through the doors. As with the library, there was an atrium, only this one wasn't overheated. The floor was flagged and there were hooks and benches either side where waterproofs and muddy boots could be left before entering the hotel proper. Only a couple were occupied. There were a pair of half-glazed French doors giving a view into a softly lit reception area beyond. When I tried them they were locked, but a young girl of about nine, with blond hair pulled into a ponytail and wearing a thick mauve sweater, saw us and skipped over and let us in.

'Hello,' she said. 'I'm Ashley. Are you the FBI lady?'

I said I was, and she ran off calling for someone called Walker.

'Ashley,' I said and looked at Boyd.

'Owner's granddaughter,' he said. 'Her parents are probably stuck the other side of Princes Ridge.'

Ashley came skipping back with a tall, thin, bespectacled man who introduced himself at Scott Walker. He had thick sandy hair brushed back and cut short, and stubble that was teetering on the edge of becoming a proper beard. Despite the woodland camouflage pants and heavy khaki sweater, he looked more like an academic on a field trip than Boyd did, although there was something dangerous about the way he moved. I got the impression he'd been in the military somewhere in his past. But then at least a third of all LEOs were estimated to be veterans. He wasn't carrying, though – not at the hip or the shoulder.

'Are you with the OJS?' I asked.

The Bureau of Indian Affairs has its own small police force – the Office of Justice Services. I'd heard that between them, the Bureau and the tribal police, jurisdiction in Indian Country could get complicated.

'Good God, no,' said Walker. 'I'm an ethnographer. I

work for the Office of Trust Services.'

'Doing what?' asked Boyd.

'Are you William Boyd?' said Walker. 'I think I know your grandfather.'

'You called the police chief,' I said, before the two men could start comparing small-town genealogies.

'The phone line is down so Ada asked me to call it in,' he said. 'She thought there were intruders trying to break into the boathouse.'

'Who's Ada?' I asked.

'Grandma,' said Ashley. 'She owns the whole hotel.'

'Ada Cole,' said Boyd, and Walker nodded.

'And she thinks she saw intruders?' I asked.

'Damn right I did,' said a voice from behind us. 'Pardon my French.'

The voice belonged to a short, smartly dressed woman in her fit fifties, with a round sun-weathered face and widely set grey eyes.

'Ada Cole,' she said, and held out a hand.

Her handshake was strong, dry, and her palm had the sort of calluses I associate with chopping your own firewood. But behind her small town self-containment I could sense tension and a fraying at the edges of her confidence. I wondered how well the hotel was doing. It certainly wasn't brimming with guests at the moment.

I asked when the incident had occurred, and Mrs Cole said she'd first seen figures down by the boathouse an hour ago but hadn't been alarmed until the exterior lights in that area went out.

'I checked the fuse box,' she said. 'But the circuit was still good, and besides, the other garden lights, which were on the same circuit, were still on.'

So she'd gone out to see what was going on and saw figures running away.

I asked in which direction, and she said toward the lower slopes of Eloise Point.

'Anything since then?' I asked.

'No,' said Mrs Cole. 'I tried calling Cameron' – the police chief – 'but the phone was dead and there was no signal on my cell – although that's not so unusual. Fortunately, that's when Walker arrived with his radio.'

That had been an hour previously, and there hadn't been any further disturbance since.

'But I haven't been out to look yet,' said Mrs Cole.

I was wondering who might be out on a freezing night like this one – apart from me, obviously – and whether they might be related to whoever broke into Patrick Henderson's house.

I said that I'd check the boathouse and the immediate grounds.

'I'll show you where everything is,' said Mrs Cole.

Shortened pump-action shotguns were obviously the must-have accessory for Wisconsin women of a certain age. Ada Cole had a businesslike and obviously well cared for Mossberg 500 that she insisted on bringing with her as we stepped out the back door of the hotel. She led the way, which was good because I'm superstitious about having armed civilians behind me.

'Be careful,' she said. 'There's a drop at the end of the patio.'

She'd turned on the floodlights that illuminated the

hotel's lakefront grounds. During the summer, Ada explained, the hotel hosted events on the patio and the lawn. As I followed Ada Cole away from the hotel, the floods picked out the nude statue on the ornamental fountain and threw our shadows ahead of us. Snowflakes fell lazily around us, deadening any sounds, so that it was as if we walked through a bubble of silence with only the crunch of our own footsteps for company.

The boathouse was a low wooden building that protruded out into the lake beside a wooden pier.

'There's supposed to be lights here, too,' said Mrs Cole. 'But they've stopped working.'

We took out our flashlights, forcing Mrs Cole to awkwardly juggle her Mossberg one-handed. She didn't have a sling for the firearm, and in the end she compromised by resting it on the crook of her elbow. Beside the boathouse, what I thought was an access road turned out to be a slipway, and the beam of my flashlight reflected off a yellow and black sign saying ICE ROAD CLOSED.

When I asked, Mrs Cole explained that the hotel had its own side access to the main ice road that ran out to Basswood Island.

'But the ice isn't thick enough yet,' she said. 'The park rangers have to certify the thickness before we can let anyone drive out.'

The clouds over the lake suddenly lit up, then flickered back to darkness, once, twice, three times. I counted one Mississippi, two Mississippi, and then heard something that sounded more like distant artillery fire than thunder. Two seconds – less than half a mile away.

'Thundersnow,' said Mrs Cole.

'Is it common?'

'Didn't used to be,' said Mrs Cole. 'But we've been getting more of it in the last couple of years. Global warming, I guess.'

We rounded the side of the boathouse and Mrs Cole swore.

There was a ragged rectangular hole where a wooden door had been ripped out of its frame. Not ripped, I realised – the door had been smashed out from the inside. Sections of the frame were splayed outward, and when I panned my flashlight around I found large fragments of the door proper spread in a cone shape away from the boathouse.

There was another lightning flash that seemed to ripple across the sky from north to south.

The remains of the doorway gaped like a broken mouth.

Thunder rolled less than a Mississippi away.

I unzipped my parka and pulled my pistol. This was going to be my second solo entry into a suspect building this evening. Not a habit a well-organised agent wants to get into.

I turned to Mrs Cole.

'Don't follow me in,' I said.

7

Being creeped out is not the same as being tactically aware. I had no reason to believe there was anything hostile in the boathouse, but it had been a long day and I wasn't about to take any chances. In movies you see people going through doorways with their firearm held out straight-armed before them. This is a recipe for having someone grab your weapon and take it away. Instead, you go in either with it close to your chest – which looks goofy, but who cares? – or down by your side with your finger safely out of the trigger guard. I chose the latter, but I held my flashlight with my thumb at the back so, if need be, I could rest my gun hand on my forearm.

It wasn't needed. I stepped smartly through the ruined doorway and shone my beam methodically into the corners, then upward, shifting position to get a view behind the wooden beams that criss-crossed the roof.

Once I'd established that nothing was about to jump me, I started to take in the details. The boathouse was a roofed dock wide enough to hold two boats side by side, with decking either side. Absent any boats, the dock had frozen over cleanly, and the beam of my flashlight shone through milky ice into the black water below. At the far end, the remains of large double doors hung brokenly from their hinges. Splinters the size of two by fours were scattered across the interior ice.

Something had smashed its way in from the lake side. Something large or powerful, or maybe both. Prior to my trip to London, I might have thought a large vehicle, or possibly explosives, but now I didn't rule anything out.

Something glistened in the beam of the flashlight and, keeping my back to the nearest wall, I edged along the right-hand dock until I could crouch down and have a closer look.

There was another flash outside, and a few seconds later the same strange muffled thunder as before. I became aware of a creeping cold sensation that was separate from the real temperature. A *vestigium* for sure, with hints of rotting vegetation and wet decay.

On the dock lay a length of torn flannel in a brown lumberjack check. I identified it as an arm torn from a shirt by the cuff at one end. It appeared to have been ripped off at the seams and, horribly, was filled from shoulder to elbow.

I thought again of the forensic team that might as well be on the far side of the moon.

'Mrs Cole,' I called without standing up. 'Don't come in yet.'

'I hear you,' she said.

'Do you have any brown paper bags back at the hotel? Unused, for preference.'

'Sure,' she said. 'What size?'

There was more lightning and muffled thunder, but I was getting used to it.

'Big ones, please, at least three,' I said. 'Call me when you get back but don't come in.'

Once she'd gone, I resumed my evidence sweep of the boathouse. There were streaks of the same glistening slime I'd spotted at Patrick Henderson's house, but only along the right-hand dock – nothing on the left.

Somebody – or something – had bashed in the lakeside doors, climbed or – terrible thought – slithered onto the right-hand dock, and then smashed its way out of the boathouse door. Why come ashore in the boathouse? Why not walk, or slither, up the slipway outside?

I squatted down at the dock and methodically swung my flashlight in a sweeping motion across the ice – taking notice of where the refraction of the beam changed. Close to where the sleeve lay was a patch of obviously thinner ice. Something shiny and rectangular reflected the light from underneath.

I looked around for anything to use to break the surface. Most of the gear had obviously been put away for the winter, but there was still a boathook hanging from hooks on the left-hand wall.

It was a long pole, so I needed both hands to handle it. I'd already holstered my firearm, but I ended up holding my flashlight between my teeth – it was not ideal. Because it was possibly evidence, I decided to start carefully at a point a foot away from the shiny rectangle. I needn't have worried. The ice proved thin and shattered with the first stab with the boathook. I cleared a section and then waited for the water to settle.

I shone my flashlight into the water and this time I could see it was definitely a smartphone. I could also see that it was sitting on top of a partially deflated inflatable boat. A large modern one in black PVC and, when I traced its length with my flashlight, a large black outboard motor. Pitched forward so I could just make out the copper gleam of its screw.

The cell phone couldn't have been more than two feet under the surface.

A decent lab can recover just about everything on a drowned phone, so I shed my parka and sweater and rolled up the sleeves of my shirt and the thermals underneath. You get blasé wearing decent cold weather gear, and I shuddered at the sudden chill as I lay down on the dock. But that was nothing compared to the shock I felt when I plunged my hand into the water.

I'd expected a delay, but my skin went numb the moment it went under. I felt my lips drawing back from my teeth as I hissed in surprise. I lunged downward grasping for the phone, and felt my numb fingertips brush its smooth face. I had to squirm forward and lean over the edge to make the extra few inches. Freezing water sloshed up my arm and soaked my rolled-up sleeves. But I got a hold of the phone.

Something brushed against my forearm – just below the elbow.

I threw myself backward, coming up in a crouch with my flashlight trained on the inky water. Something pale and organic flashed in the beam and then vanished from sight.

Fish, I thought desperately. *You get fish in lakes.*

I was trembling, but it might have been the cold.

Definitely a fish, I said to myself. *Also, not climbing out of the water after me.*

I checked my prize – it looked like an iPhone 5.

I heard Boyd calling my name from outside.

'Have you got the bags?' I called back.

'Right here,' called Mrs Cole.

I looked over to the ruined doorway, which was filled with white light. Somebody had thought to bring a portable lamp. I kicked myself because it hadn't been me. I told them they could come in providing they stayed close to the wall.

Pins and needles started randomly prickling in my hand and forearm. I guessed that the water under the dock must have been much colder than I'd thought. I dried my arm on the outside of my parka and unrolled my sleeves. By the time I had my parka back on, Boyd and Mrs Cole had arrived.

'Is that an arm?' asked Boyd, staring at the sleeve on the floor.

Mrs Cole held out open a paper bag, the kind you pack groceries in, for me to drop the phone in.

'I hope not,' I said, but I thought it probably was.

The sleeve came off the dock in one frozen lump that at least made it easy to wrestle into another grocery bag.

'Fuck,' said Mrs Cole, when she noticed the smashed lakeside doors for the first time. 'What in Christ's name did that?'

I winced and wished silently that people wouldn't curse like that.

'A boat?' said Boyd. 'Had to have been a boat.'

Once I had the sleeve and the phone safely bagged, I

had Boyd hold the LPG lamp over the patch I'd cleared in the ice while I poked around with the boathook. I asked Mrs Cole if she owned an inflatable, but she said no.

'And we had to sell the boats five years ago,' she said.

The hotel had maintained a pair of boats that guests could rent for fishing trips or to sail over to the Apostle Islands National Lakeshore.

'Then there was the crash and things got tight,' she said. 'I couldn't afford the upkeep any more and the damn things depreciate like nobody's business, so I sold them off.' She sighed and looked around the boathouse – wincing again at the ruins of the doors. 'I hope the insurance covers that.'

'Tell them it was storm damage,' said Boyd. 'I'll back you up.'

There was no sign of a storm as we stepped back out the ruined door and the snow seemed lighter. I sent Mrs Cole back to the hotel with the evidence, but not before asking to borrow her Mossberg.

'Do you know how to use one of these?' I asked Boyd.

'Only on tin cans,' he said, but didn't object when I handed it over. He had enough firearm awareness to check the safety button and hold it with the barrel pointing away from me.

I grabbed the gas lantern and we set out across the snow-covered grounds. Mrs Cole had reported seeing figures running from the boathouse toward Eloise Point, so we headed in that direction. The wind had dropped to nothing and the snow fell in eerie silence. I walked slowly, zigzagging slightly to cover the widest possible path. Snow would have covered any tracks, but there were enough walls, hedges and other obstacles that might have caught an unwary intruder – especially one moving quickly at night.

'What are we looking for?' asked Boyd. 'And are you really expecting me to shoot someone?'

'I don't know,' I said, 'and hopefully not.'

We saw the blood before we saw the body. It showed as a black stain in the white glare from the lantern, soaked into the snow on the far side of an ornamental hedge, which explained why it hadn't been covered up. Poking out of an adjacent snowbank was a hoof. It was large, two-toed, and probably a deer. This I confirmed by partially digging it out the bank. The limb terminated at the knee, the skin and muscle ragged – suggesting it had been torn away. It was cold to the touch, but the blood spatter under it suggested it had happened fairly recently.

'That's not how I'd dress a deer,' said Boyd. 'Could have been a wolf attack.'

'Is that common up here?' I asked.

'Not that I've heard,' he said, but I noticed that he brought the barrel of the Mossberg up and looked around carefully.

I asked what was up ahead.

'Eloise Point,' he said, and once he pointed it out I could see the hill as a darker patch of night vanishing into the low clouds.

There was no fence or hedge, but it was easy to see where the hotel grounds ended and the woods began. I considered trying to pick up a trail among the trees, where the snow might be less thick, but came to my senses.

'Back to the hotel,' I said.

'Are we taking the venison with us?' he asked.

'No,' I said. 'The crime scene team can dig it up when they get here.'

'You think it's connected to the break-in?'

I thought of the deer's head I'd found near Patrick Henderson's house.

'I think it's all connected,' I said. 'I just don't know how.'

8

The hotel had a large commercial kitchen fitted with easy-to-clean stainless steel sinks and preparation areas. Mrs Cole suggested putting the cell phone in a cup full of rice, but Boyd said it was better to use the silica desiccation sachets of the kind he kept in his instrument case. While he went to grab them, I removed the sleeve from its bag and laid it out on a stainless steel baking tray that Mrs Cole pulled from a cupboard.

'That definitely looks like somebody's arm to me,' Boyd said when he returned.

'No shit, Sherlock,' said Mrs Cole.

Once he'd handed over the desiccation sachets, he asked if it was all right if he ran up to the weather station on Eloise Point.

'Sure,' I said. 'Can you come back and give me a lift back to the library?'

'Sure,' he said, and hesitated at the kitchen door. 'Right,' he said after a moment before turning and leaving.

'Oh,' said Mrs Cole after he was safely gone. 'I think you've made an impression there.'

I felt my cheeks heat, but told myself it was a delayed reaction to getting out of the cold.

I told Mrs Cole that she'd better find Ashley and make sure she didn't wander into the kitchen.

'I'm going to have a quick look and see what we have here,' I said. 'I don't want her trying to sneak a peek.'

'What are you expecting to find?'

'I don't know,' I said. 'Hopefully it's just an arm.'

Mrs Cole hesitated, and I could tell she wanted to ask what the hell else I thought I might find. But obviously she decided against it. Once she was out of the kitchen, I pulled on a pair of purple latex gloves and carefully peeled back some of the cloth on the item. It had adhered to whatever was in the sleeve, but I detached enough to identify that what it was sticking to *was* a human upper arm. It had obviously been ripped off below the shoulder joint, and I couldn't see a bone, but there was a suggestion of a hole where the humerus might have fitted. It had belonged to a Caucasian adult – I wanted to say male because it was large and well-muscled, but that would be an assumption.

'What have you got there?' asked Scott Walker from behind me.

I started. I hadn't heard him come in.

I let him look.

'Male Caucasian,' he said. 'Adult, probably under forty.'

'Anyone you recognise?'

He laughed.

'I generally prefer to have a bit more to go on,' he said. 'If I'm making an identification.'

'Are you sure you're not law enforcement?' I asked.

'This isn't my first body part,' he said. 'Although usually they're much older.'

'Is that what you do in Indian Country?' I said. 'Dig up bodies?'

'That's archaeologists,' he said. 'But as the only ethnographer for a hundred miles, you'd be surprised by what I get asked to look at.'

I considered peeling back more cloth to see if I could find a distinguishing mark – a tattoo would be too much to ask for – but decided against it. I figured I could wait for the forensic team to arrive. Figured wrong, as it happened, but I wasn't to know that at the time.

As I slipped the arm back into its grocery bag, I asked Scott Walker what he knew about local history.

'A lot, actually,' he said. 'You can't know a people without knowing their history.'

'What do you know about the Marsh expedition of 1843?' I asked. 'The one that was supposed to have made winter camp in Eloise and then went missing.'

'Oh yeah,' he said, pronouncing it 'ya' in the Wisconsin style. 'Right on this very spot. The hotel is supposed to be built on the campsite.'

'What? Really?'

'Definitely,' he said. 'As far as we know.'

'Do you know what happened to them? The Marsh expedition.'

'They all died.'

'As far as you know.'

'As far as we know.'

People don't have nearly as good control of their facial expressions as they think they do. However casual he tried to act, his eyes betrayed a sudden intense interest before he looked away to the left.

I had been about to tell him about the journal, but something in his manner made me hesitate.

'So what do you think happened to them?' I asked.

'I think they succumbed to the harsh conditions,' he said. 'It wasn't that uncommon.'

I watched as he wandered across the kitchen and started opening cupboards.

'Would you like a hot chocolate?' he said, pulling a catering-sized can of Swiss Miss instant from the cupboard. 'There's even marshmallows.'

He turned and waved a packet of Jet-Puffed Marshmallows at me. He seemed extremely comfortable and easy in what was, after all, somebody else's kitchen.

'Thanks,' I said. 'What about local legends?'

'About the 1843 expedition? Nothing in particular.'

He filled a kettle; the metallic sound of the water sloshing inside echoed in the big kitchen.

'What about on the reservation?'

Scott clanged the kettle onto a burner on the big range.

'Do they have any legends about the way it went missing?' I asked.

'You need to be careful about how you use the word "legend",' he said. 'It's not always appropriate.'

He was changing the subject, but I went along. It was exactly like talking to Cymbeline – all you had to do was keep the conversation going and, sooner or later, they would tell you what you wanted to know.

Assuming that they knew something. But I was pretty sure Scott Walker knew something.

'In what way?' I asked.

'People talk about Native American legends when they're really talking about Native religious practices and beliefs,' he said. 'I'll just bet you're a Christian.'

'Aren't you?'

'Born Anabaptist,' he said. 'And I've even been known to go to church on special occasions.'

'I'm a Christian,' I said.

'And you believe that Jesus Christ is your Lord and saviour?'

'With all my heart,' I said. 'Does that surprise you?'

The kettle whistled and Scott started clattering around – making the hot chocolate.

'No,' he said. 'Not really. And do you think that the crucifixion was a real event, and that Christ died for our sins and rose on the third day?'

'Yes.'

'So not a legend but a truth?' he said.

'Yes,' I said, and because I could see the obvious direction of that comparison, I thought we'd skip the smug self-righteousness phase of the conversation.

'Are there any local *traditions* that relate to the missing expedition?'

'There's a story, but it doesn't come from the rez,' he said, and then made me wait while he sprinkled marshmallows into the cups. Four cups, I noticed, enough for Ashley and Mrs Cole.

'There's an account by a French Canadian trapper dating back to about the right time,' he said. 'Tells of an official American government expedition that foolishly accepted guidance from a trickster spirit in the shape of a wolf, who lured them out onto the ice. Once they were far from their camp, he summoned up all his family – also wolves, I might add – who fell upon the expedition and tore them to pieces.'

'Wolf spirits?' I said.

'*Espirit loup*,' he said. 'I found the account while researching hunting patterns around the Great Lakes.' It had been in the LAC, the Library and Archives Canada, in Ottawa. 'I was looking for wolves and found wolf spirits instead.'

He brought me one of the mugs.

'Do you believe in wolf spirits?' I asked.

He stopped in front of me and his eyes narrowed.

'Exactly why are you here, Agent Reynolds?' he asked.

'I'm looking for Patrick Henderson,' I said.

He handed me my hot chocolate.

'Did he find something?' asked Walker.

That was a giveaway. He was trying to sound casual, but he'd skipped the whole 'what's good old Patrick got to do with the price of soya' step of the conversation. I was even more sure he knew something now.

'What do you think he might have found?' I asked.

He held my eyes for a long moment, but then turned back to the counter.

'We need to have a chat,' he said.

I sipped my hot chocolate as he picked up two mugs and took them out the kitchen. He'd been skimpy on the marshmallows, I noticed.

When you're working a case what you want is facts.

You might not know what they mean or how they fit together, but they anchor your case to the real world. My facts so far were that Patrick Henderson had called the Bureau and warned us that a situation with *unusual characteristics* might be developing. This morning, while I was en route to meet him, he left his home, possibly not of his own free will. At the same time, an extremely rare – and, according to Boyd, unusually powerful – snow tornado had come ashore, flattening the town hall and making a beeline for Henderson's house.

His neighbour, Rhonda Macklewright, may or may not have seen him dragged off by a group of people, some of whom may have sported horns. Although, alternatively, they may have been carrying the head of a deer with them.

Prior to calling the Bureau, Henderson had read the journal of Ephraim Wright of Poughkeepsie, which gave an account of how the bulk of the Marsh expedition were led away from their camp by a friendly Native American.

Had this been the *Espirit Loup* – the wolf spirit recorded in the account by the Canadian trapper? Ephraim's journal didn't mention anything about wolves, and it was a primary source written by an eyewitness, not a 'tradition' passed on second-hand.

And Henderson had explicitly warned Sadie Clarkson, the librarian, not to show it to anyone. Who had Henderson been worried about reading it, and why? I had to work on the assumption that the journal had to do with the situation with unusual characteristics that Henderson had called about.

I needed facts, and there was one I could confirm straight away. I finished my hot chocolate – not bad, a seven out of ten – and went over to where the drowned iPhone was sitting in a wooden serving box with Boyd's desiccation sachets. I lifted it carefully up to my ear and gave it a gentle shake – nothing.

My parka was still hanging on the hooks by the back door and I retrieved my screwdriver set from the inside pocket. I carry a set of small screwdrivers, including the pentalobe one, for just the purpose of opening phones. Exposure to magic – and it still seems strange to use that word in cold blood – can seriously damage micro-processors, so checking phones has become a routine crime scene diagnostic.

I was levering off the top of the iPhone when Scott Walker walked back in. He came over to the table and raised an eyebrow when he saw what I was doing. Once more he was trying to look blandly quizzical, but there was a definite tension about the way he was holding himself.

The motherboard was to the right of the battery, and I didn't need to prise out the main chip because I could see where glittering sand had leaked out into the casing before being glued down with water.

This is what my British colleague Peter Grant calls 'sanding'. And it only gets this bad when there's been massive amounts of magic nearby.

Walker bent over to look closely and then raised his head to meet my gaze.

'Do you know what this means?' he asked.

'That you're not a damned ethnographer,' I said.

9

'I am too,' said Walker. 'Graduated magna cum laude from Penn School of Anthropology.'

'Are you a practitioner?' I asked, because it had been a long day, and anyhow I don't find verbal sparring that entertaining.

'No,' he said. 'Are you?'

'No. But you know what "practitioner" means.'

'Wizard,' he said, surprising me. 'Or would you prefer magic user?'

'I'd prefer a straight answer,' I said.

Walker stepped back and folded his arms.

'I work for the Office of Trust Service,' he said. 'And my principal duty is to assist the tribal authorities in preserving their social and material cultural matrix. They've lost so much, we can't afford to lose what we have left.'

'What *we* have left?'

'It's our legacy, too,' he said. 'As much a part of American culture as life, liberty and the pursuit of a good cheeseburger.'

'And that includes magic?'

'Before we get to that,' he said, 'what do you know about magic?'

'I've seen it in action,' I said.

He tilted his head.

'Where?' he asked.

'In London, England,' I said.

'OK,' he said. 'That I can believe.'

'So *are* there Native American practitioners?'

'You have to understand that what I'm about to say is a generalisation,' he said. 'There's a great deal of diversity among the tribes and nations, so it doesn't apply across the board.'

I nodded and he continued.

'We know from various sources that many tribal religious practices had a demonstrable effect,' he said.

Not earth-shattering effects, he explained, but enough to improve hunting and medicine, and what Walker called 'general quality of life'.

'Then there are the spirits,' he said. 'Although the exact relationship between them and the tribes is disputed.'

Disputed by whom? I wondered. Had Walker ever actually met one of these spirits? I'd met some strange people in the tunnels under London, and my English friend Peter was cohabiting with a woman he reliably informed me was a river goddess.

I wondered what Walker's reaction to that particular revelation would be? I try to be open and straightforward with my fellow law enforcement, be they ever so humble, but I wasn't sure what Scott Walker was *really*. And I certainly didn't think he was being straightforward with me.

'Many of these spirits were hostile to American

expansion and had to be forcibly pacified,' he said. 'But magic was not a factor in any of the conflicts with tribal Indians until the British intervened during the war of 1812. They directly aided Tecumseh's Confederacy, supplying muskets and powder and – more insidiously – they found a way to weaponise Native religious practice.'

And once the genie was out of the bottle, there was no putting it back in. Thanks to the British, the US Government was forced to organise its own magical cadres to deal with the threat.

'And even after the British were defeated, the threat remained,' said Walker. 'The government couldn't allow potentially hostile practitioners a chance to wreak havoc on the frontier. We had no choice but to target medicine men, which, sadly, did untold damage to tribal culture.'

He seemed genuinely upset by this.

'And now?' I asked.

'These days we take a more balanced approach,' he said. 'We try to work with the tribal authorities and the practitioners themselves. Persuade them that it's in their and their people's best interests if they limit their activities to the reservations.'

'"We" being the BIA?'

'Yes, since 1824,' he said. 'As part of our original charter.'

'But not the OJS?'

The Office of Justice Service, who ran the Bureau of Indian Affairs' law enforcement wing.

'That's a whole different set of problems,' he said. 'As I told you, I'm with the Office of Trust Services.'

'But you served in some capacity?' I asked, because his whole manner was too crisp and too watchful for him not to have been a badge.

'Air Force OSI out of Wright-Patt,' he said.

The Office of Special Investigation was the crime-fighting branch of the Air Force's security forces. And an odd choice of career for someone with a degree in anthropology. Which I pointed out.

'Went straight in at eighteen,' he said. 'Stayed in for eight, then I went to Penn.'

'And then the BIA?'

'Actually, they sponsored the degree,' he said.

Something was bugging me. Usually when you get into the 'where did you serve?' conversation the other party expects you to reciprocate, but Walker hadn't asked – hadn't shown any curiosity at all.

Which probably meant he knew all about me already. Which would mean he'd looked me up or been briefed about me before he'd arrived in Eloise. Which meant someone told him I was coming yesterday. However, given that I'd liaised with the local field office, the county sheriff's department and the Eloise PD, any number of people might have called up Walker and told him I was on my way.

Heck, it was even a legitimate thing to do, given Walker's job and the proximity of the Red Cliff Reservation.

Hi, Scott. Washington's sending up some damn Fed, know anything about her?

I swear inter-agency co-operation was a great deal more straightforward when I was doing fraud cases out of Albany. I really don't like this kind of bullpucky, so I decided to level with Walker and told him all about the phone call from Henderson.

'He really called it an "X-RAY SIERRA INDIA" situation?' asked Walker.

'You know what that means?' I asked.

'I've seen it referenced in files relating back to the unrest of the 1970s,' he said. 'But I never found an explanation. Do you know what it means?'

My boss, Assistant Director Harris, had associated XSI with the 1990s – did it go further back?

'Only that a case might be UC,' I said. 'Have unusual characteristics.'

Walker gave a mirthless bark of laughter.

'Not much more than I knew already,' he said.

Sometimes you have to give a little to get information, especially when dealing with other agencies.

'Do you know about the journal?' I asked.

'What journal?'

So I told him about Ephraim Wright of Poughkeepsie, his journal, and his account of how a young Native man had led the bulk of the Marsh expedition off over the ice – never to return.

'Where is it?' asked Walker.

'Could this have been your wolf spirit?'

'What?'

Walker pulled himself back from wherever his thought processes had gone.

'Maybe,' he said. 'But there was an Ojibwe winter village where the waterfront is now. It might have been a friendly, looking to help or make a trade.'

You don't believe that, I thought. *You believe it was a wolf spirit, or at the very least an* unfriendly.

'Do you have the journal with you?' he asked.

'I left it back at the library,' I said. 'But it's evidence in an ongoing inquiry.'

Walker looked like he wanted to say something, but changed his mind. He shook his head ruefully.

'I'm concerned that we might have a situation here,' he said, and then paused as if picking his next words carefully. 'We could be dealing with a malignant spirit.'

'Have you ever encountered one personally?'

He shook his head.

'I've read accounts from the turn of the century,' he said. 'There was trouble around Leech Lake in Minnesota, and reports of an unnatural creature that was set loose upon the army and the National Guard.'

'Set loose?'

'Deliberately set loose by Chippewa medicine men.' Walker looked uncomfortable. 'So the reports say. What is certain is that a creature described as "an unholy marriage of stag and man" fought agents of the US Government.'

I thought of the deer's head I'd found on Patrick Henderson's street, and Rhonda Macklewright's initial report of antlers and muzzles. And then I thought of the detached arm on the tray beside me and the deer's leg I'd found outside in the hotel grounds. I had a brief nostalgic pang for my early career, where I could trust my fellow law enforcers and didn't worry about weird creatures out of mythology.

'Who were the agents?' I asked.

'Not us,' said Walker. 'All I could find out was they were based in Charlottesville, Virginia.'

I thought I might know who these Virginian gentlemen might be, but I decided to keep that to myself until I could be sure.

'My concern,' said Walker, 'is that such a weaponised spirit may have been set upon the 1843 expedition and then lain dormant until now. Since it was created, so to speak, as a weapon against white settlement, it may be carrying out that purpose now.'

'A hundred and seventy years later?' I said. 'Why start now?'

'Who knows?' said Walker. 'Global warming, fracking, a change in the alignment of the stars—' He stopped suddenly and turned as if he'd heard something. 'Did you hear that?'

I shook my head and we both listened.

There was the hum of the big refrigerator by the sinks and – on the other side of the door – running feet. Then Ashley burst in, brandishing something silver in one hand.

'Scott, Scott!' she yelled. 'Look what I found!'

As she rushed over to Scott, I took the opportunity to throw a dish towel over the severed arm and stand so I was between it and Ashley. Not that she was looking my way, being far too intent on showing a silver disc to Walker. She stuck her pinkie through a hole in its centre and I saw that it was a silver dollar.

'Can I see?' asked Walker, and Ashley handed the coin over.

Walker gave it a careful examination while Ashley

bounced up and down on her heels. He frowned suddenly, as if recognising something unpleasant, but quickly quashed the expression in favour of cheerful interest.

'Is it rare?' asked Ashley.

'It's certainly rare,' said Walker. 'I think it's a Gobrecht silver dollar. See – it says 1836 on the edge.'

'Is it valuable?' asked Ashley. 'Will it help Grandma?'

'You might want to show it to an expert in a museum,' said Walker. 'The edges of the hole have been carefully smoothed – feel.'

He held out the coin so that Ashley could feel the edges of the hole.

'That means it might have been worn as a medallion or strung with beads to make a necklace.'

'Is it Native American?' asked Ashley.

Walker gasped and suddenly looked briefly shocked.

'Sorry?' he said to Ashley after a moment. 'What was the question?'

Ashley repeated herself.

'It might have been, or it might have belonged to an early settler,' said Walker. 'Where did you find it?'

'It was out front,' said Ashley. 'When I was clearing snow off the stairs.'

'When was this?' Walker's tone was sharper, I think, than he meant it to be, and Ashley's expression turned mulish.

'This morning,' she said. 'Before you came. Give it back.'

Walker hesitated, and then handed the coin back to Ashley, who clutched it tightly in her fist. Walker made a concerted effort to be pleasant.

'Can you show me where you found it?' he said.

'Why?' asked Ashley.

'There might be more coins?' I said.

While we got into our parkas and gloves, I persuaded Ashley to let me handle the coin. It was much heavier than a modern coin, and as soon as I touched it I felt its *vestigium* – a smoky sensation. Faint, but unmistakably complex, like a melody made from the sound of snow falling and water lapping a shore. It wasn't the most powerful *vestigium* I'd ever felt, but it was the most intricate.

And then a shock like a stab in the chest with an icicle. I gasped, just as Walker had.

Ashley frowned and held out her hand.

I handed Ashley back her prize before she could start growling, pulled on my gloves, and followed her out the front entrance and down the steps.

'There.'

Ashley pointed to a patch of snow-covered gravel between Walker's Cherokee and what I assumed would be flower beds come the spring thaw.

Walker reached into the flatbed of his Cherokee and pulled out a snow shovel. And started methodically turning over the snow. He seemed very intent, and so I left him to it and raised the gas lamp high to augment the softer light from the hotel porch lamps.

There was no breeze at all now and the snow had all but ceased – just the occasional fat flake falling straight down.

Lightning lit the clouds behind the hotel, over the lake. I counted until the muffled thunder. Six seconds

– so just over a mile away. I didn't know whether that meant another storm front was pushing in or not. There's never a good-looking meteorologist around when you need one.

'Find anything?' I asked Walker and Ashley.

'Not yet,' said Walker, who was widening his search along the front of the buried flower bed.

I suddenly desperately wanted to know who had been the last set of visitors to have stayed at the hotel. Mrs Cole was the obvious person to ask, but there was no way I was leaving Walker or Ashley out here alone. So I asked Ashley, just in case she knew. Which, amazingly, she did.

'That was Mr. Bunker,' she said. 'Who skipped town without paying his bill. Grandma had to report him to the chief and everything.'

When I asked when they'd last seen Mr. Bunker, she said it was before Christmas.

'He said he'd be coming back after,' said Ashley.

Mr. Bunker had taken his room at the start of December and negotiated a good long-term rate until the end of January.

'Grandma didn't like that, but she said she needed the business,' said Ashley. 'And he wasn't trouble.'

Because he was used to going off for a couple of days at a time before coming back and asking if he could do all his laundry. That's why they hadn't been worried about his absence until the day before yesterday. They didn't need the room for anything else, and he wasn't even using up the soap while he was away.

Lightning flashed, brighter this time and less than

three seconds away. I felt the hairs on the back of my neck rise.

'Did he say where he went on these trips?' I asked.

'He said exploring,' said Ashley. 'He wanted to visit the islands before the lake froze.'

Walker stopped shovelling and straightened up.

'Did he say which island?' he asked.

'Nope,' said Ashley.

I was thinking of the sunken inflatable in the boat-house. And of the human arm I had defrosting in the kitchen.

'We're not going to find anything tonight,' said Walker, and threw the snow shovel back into the bed of the pickup.

Ashley made a little sound of disappointment.

'We can . . .' started Walker, but just then all the lights inside and outside the hotel went out.

10

'Inside!' I said.

'It's just the power,' said Ashley. 'Goes out all the time.'

'Inside,' I said, and, unzipping my parka, drew my pistol.

Ashley stared wide-eyed at the gun, and then at Walker, who took her hand and led her up the stairs. I followed them up, pausing at the top to turn and scan the hotel grounds. It took a long nerve-racking moment for my eyes to adjust to the darkness, and even then the world was reduced to varied textures of black.

I saw nothing, but I could feel a creeping wrongness, like a cold finger brushing down my spine. A couple of years previously I would have put the sensation down to nerves but now I knew better. This was a *vestigium*. But Peter Grant had never told me that it could encompass an entire landscape. Or feel so inimical.

'Grant, O Lord, Thy protection,' I said, and retreated until the door was at my back. 'And in protection, strength. And in strength, understanding.'

Then I slipped inside and slammed the bolts top and bottom.

It was a prayer I'd liked as a kid, because from

understanding comes knowledge, and from knowledge, the knowledge of justice . . . and from that, the love of justice, and from that, the love of all existences. I'd actually recited it the morning I set off for my Phase One assessment test – my first proper step to joining the FBI.

I found it surprisingly comforting in the darkness of the hotel's porch, though the weight of my Glock 22 in my hand was, as always, a more immediate reassurance. Light flared behind me and I backed into the lobby, where Walker was holding the gas lamp in his left hand, and an extremely unacademic semi-automatic pistol in his right.

With proper trigger discipline, I saw, hand down by his side, finger out of the guard. Obviously his air force training had stuck.

Ashley's face peered over the reception counter – an oval of excited dismay.

'Did you see anything?' asked Walker.

'I want Grandma,' said Ashley in a flat matter-of-fact tone.

'I'm here, dear,' said Mrs Cole, striding in from the back office. 'Whatever is the matter?' She saw the guns and frowned. 'Agent Reynolds?'

'Just a precaution,' I said. 'Do you have a backup generator?'

Mrs Cole found that funny. Of course she had a backup generator – every business in town did. I asked where it was located.

'In the basement,' said Mrs Cole.

I pulled out my flashlight and tossed it to Walker.

'You two, go and get it going,' I said. 'And stay together.'

Walker hesitated, but then nodded and turned to Mrs Cole.

'Let's go,' he said.

'I need to turn off the floodlights first,' said Mrs Cole. 'It doesn't have enough juice to run the exterior lights.'

'We'll do that on the way,' said Walker, and they headed out the back of the lobby.

That left me with Ashley, who still had the gas lamp. She glanced the way her grandma had gone and then back at me.

'Do you know what your grandma did with Mr. Bunker's luggage?' I asked.

'It's still in the room,' she said. 'Grandma said there was no point moving it since it wasn't like we were short of space.'

Counting on an obvious tendency toward curiosity, I asked whether she knew which room it had been. Of course she did, and what's more, she knew where a spare master key was. As a reward, I let her follow me into Mr. Bunker's room – although only after I'd checked it was empty.

They were nice rooms, if a bit old-fashioned. I'd got to be a bit of a connoisseur of hotel rooms during my last assignment, and this was a step up from the places I'd stayed on the Bureau's budget. A large double bed with a geometric green and pink patterned bedspread, a flat-screen TV, fake antique desk and leather chair, prints of mountains, forests and lakes.

I searched the fridge first and found it well stocked,

but nothing was hidden behind the miniature bottles or inside the tiny freezer. There was also nothing under the bed, although Ashley couldn't stop giggling as I got down on my belly to look.

I checked the small but scrupulously clean bathroom, and found that Mr. Bunker had left a toiletry bag with an electric razor and aftershave lotion inside beside the sink. The razor was sleek and black and expensive-looking – something told me that Mr. Bunker had definitely planned on returning.

My initial sweep complete, that left the battered black four-wheeler case that had been neatly stowed in the closet. I pulled it out and laid it on the bed and used my pocketknife to force the lock.

'Should you be doing that?' asked Ashley.

'I'm worried for Mr. Bunker's safety,' I said.

Inside were neatly folded – and clean – check shirts, underpants, undershirts, and a grey zip-up pouch made of ballistic fabric with Smith & Wesson embossed on the front.

'What's that?' asked Ashley.

'Pistol bag,' I said.

I could tell from the weight that it was empty, but I unzipped it and turned it out just in case. Nothing useful emerged. I unzipped the divider on the inside of the front shell of the suitcase and found four plain manilla folders. They were crumpled and looked like they'd been stuffed untidily into the compartment. There was a brown stain on one of them that smelled of coffee. I laid them out on the bed and Ashley positioned the lamp so I could read their contents. The first folder I opened contained high-resolution orbital photographs of a series of islands.

'That's the Apostles,' said Ashley.

There were no markings or labels on the pictures, but they looked a little too crisp and detailed to be off Google Maps. From the NRO – National Reconnaissance Office – at a guess. Although I couldn't rule out a foreign agency, or even a private contractor.

One complication at a time, I told myself.

The second folder was a hard copy of Patrick Henderson's FBI file, the same one I'd accessed back at Quantico. I quickly leafed through it and saw there were additional pages, but I didn't think I had time to check them immediately.

The third folder was a similar, but much slimmer, official-looking personnel file – only this one was for Scott Walker. It confirmed his position in the BIA as an ethnographer in the Office of Trust Services, and listed projects he'd worked on in and around various reservations in the Great Lakes region. Plus, I saw, a bibliography of books he'd published on pre-Columbian Ojibwe culture. There was nothing in the file to indicate that he'd trained as a magical practitioner, or even taken an academic interest in the subject.

The fourth folder contained a different type of dossier, but also a familiar one. It consisted of a series of pictures of Sadie Clarkson, the Eloise public librarian, and a printed summary of publicly available information about her, gleaned from social media and the like. The pictures showed her entering and leaving the library and other buildings that might have been in and around Eloise. Judging by the angles and the heavy use of a long lens, these were clandestine surveillance images. There were several more pictures with the unmistakable old-fashioned balconied row houses of New Orleans' French Quarter.

'That's Miss Clarkson,' said Ashley.

I really shouldn't have been letting the girl read over my shoulder, but she was handy holding the lamp, and at least this way I knew where she was.

'Did she come down to the hotel often?'

Ashley screwed up her face in thought.

'No,' she said. 'But she came to school and did reading lessons. She said any of us could be special and not know it. And she read us this book about wizards.'

'Harry Potter?'

'No,' said Ashley. '*A Wizard of Earthsea.*'

The lights were still out. Surely it couldn't take that long to spark up a generator – not in a well-organised business like this one?

'Shall we go find your grandma?' I said, and Ashley nodded.

I stuffed the folders under my sweater, tucking them into my belt. It wasn't comfortable, but I was sure I didn't want Scott Walker knowing about his file until I'd had a chance to read it thoroughly.

I thought I heard a noise outside in the corridor so, gesturing to Ashley to stay put, I eased the room door open. I stood and listened.

Behind me Ashley fidgeted, and I was about to start moving when I heard something. It was muffled and coming from the direction of the foyer. It sounded like shouting, angry shouting. I took my pistol in one hand and Ashley's hand in the other and quietly led her out into the corridor.

Ashley started to speak but I shushed her.

Beyond the blue-white ring of light from the lamp, the hotel corridor disappeared rapidly into darkness. I needed all my senses, but all I could hear was Ashley's breathing, and all I could feel was the trembling of her hand in mine and my own heartbeat.

Angling my left arm so that Ashley stayed behind me, we advanced down the corridor toward the central part of the hotel. We had just reached the fire door that separated us from the foyer when there was a crash behind us.

It was unmistakably a window breaking.

I turned and pushed Ashley behind me.

There was a thump from inside one of the rooms up the corridor, then the sound of breaking furniture, and then a massive blow against the inside of one of the doors. It shook the frame enough for me to see that it was the room we'd just come from.

Another blow, and the sound of cracking wood.

I raised my pistol.

A third blow broke the door, and I saw splinters fly across the width of the corridor.

For a moment, everything was silent and still.

Then the lights came on.

'Oh, goodie,' said Ashley, and I exhaled.

Something large, white and impossible smashed through the door and turned to face us.

11

One of my instructors at Quantico once told me that they weren't training us to act on instinct, but liberating our minds so we could make rational decisions.

'You may only have a split second to make a fire/don't fire decision,' she'd said. 'And, believe me, at the point of decision you *will* be highly stressed. Our aim here is to make the mechanics of aiming, firing and gun safety totally automatic. So that when you find yourself in the terrible situation of having to draw your weapon in anger, not one scintilla of your brain power will be devoted to *how* to fire – only on whether or not to fire.'

I do not think my instructor had the scenario I was facing in mind.

The figure in the corridor was as tall as a man and looked like a decayed snowman with antlers. When it moved I caught glimpses of fur, sinew and bone working underneath an outer layer of dirty snow. There were no eyes, and only a horizontal slash for a mouth filled with sharp yellowing spikes. It turned its head from side to side, as if using the antlers that erupted from its head like radar to zero in.

My instinct was to open fire, but it was entirely possible that this was a man in a really strange costume.

There was no weapon visible, unless it was under the snow where the hands should be. I had to proceed on the assumption that this was a human being.

'FBI!' I shouted in the command voice I'd been taught by the same instructor. 'Don't move!'

The creature stopped moving, which was a hopeful sign.

'Turn around slowly and put your hands on top of your head,' I said, suppressing a crazy urge to tell it to interlace its fingers with its antlers.

Then there was that subtle shift in the shoulders and the hips that said co-operation would not be forthcoming.

I started to tell Ashley to back up through the fire door, but before I could get her name out of my mouth, the decaying snowman charged.

'Freeze!' I yelled as loud as I could, but the thing lumbered toward us, slow at first but picking up speed.

I put three rounds into the centre mass, saw white puffs fountain snow to reveal green and red viscera beneath. Then fired another two rounds when the figure didn't even slow down.

This is a good grouping, by the way. According to my instructors, 80 per cent of all rounds fired by LEOs miss their target.

I've been in a couple of difficult situations before where I've found it useful to ask myself, 'What would Peter Grant say?' Not 'What would he do?' because I'm never going to be that desperate. But his advice has proved useful in the past. And he is the only practising magician I actually trust.

What I think Peter would have said in that situation would be: 'Kimberley, stop shooting the fudging snowman, it obviously doesn't care, and get the fudge out of there.'

The good thing about fire doors is they're supposed to open easily in both directions. I scooped up Ashley in my left arm, turned and shouldered my way through the door. She squealed and dropped the lamp.

She was a sturdy child, so I staggered rather than ran into the foyer.

Almost straight into Mrs Cole who, praise Jesus, had her shotgun. Behind her was Scott Walker, also armed. Both were staring at what was coming up behind us.

'What the fuck?' said Walker.

As I half-threw Ashley in Walker's direction, Mrs Cole raised her shotgun.

'The legs!' I shouted, wishing I was the one holding the Mossberg.

But may the Lord bless country grandmas. She didn't even hesitate, just readjusted her aim and blew the monster's left leg off at the knee. Then there was a click-clack as she reloaded and did the same to the right.

The thing looked almost comical as it fell face first onto the floor.

Then it threw out its arms and started to drag itself toward us. I could see fingers made of what might have been muscle mixed with fur and sticks and ivy, digging into the hotel carpet, the better to pull it forward.

As we backed away, there was a crash behind us and Ashley screamed.

I turned in time to see Walker open fire with his own

semi-automatic. He was aiming at another snow monster; this one was smaller and lower to the ground and on all fours. Its head was a single gaping maw ringed with rows of teeth, like a leech.

Walker was aiming for the legs, but they were smaller and faster moving than the snowman's. Beside me, Mrs Cole blasphemed and fired again, blowing an antler off the crawling snowman. Black and green fluid splashed across the carpet, but the thing kept on crawling.

In my head, Peter Grant said in an old-fashioned English accent, *Perhaps now would be an opportune moment to depart.*

Sometimes I really hate the British – even when they're imaginary.

Mrs Cole was pulling shells from the pockets of her slacks and reloading the Mossberg. Ashley had stopped screaming because the horrible snow dog had stopped moving. Walker had his pistol trained down the opposite corridor. There was definitely movement at the far end.

Now, I decided, was a good time to take imaginary Peter Grant's advice.

'Mr. Walker!' I called. 'Check out the front.'

He nodded and ran for the front entrance.

I held out my hand for the Mossberg and Mrs Cole hesitated for a long second before handing it over. Then, without prompting, she took Ashley's hand and drew her into the atrium. I saw her grabbing overcoats as she hustled her granddaughter out the front.

I checked down both the north and south corridors. There was movement at the end of both. I considered running for the kitchen to retrieve the severed arm, but just then things came boiling up the corridors from both directions.

I considered opening fire for a moment – a very short moment – and then I went running out the front door, thankful that I'd kept my parka on indoors.

Walker was already behind the wheel of his pickup, and Mrs Cole was climbing into the cab behind Ashley. As I headed over, the engine started and the headlights temporarily blinded me. Walker gunned it, spinning the wheels in the snow.

I heard him cursing as he changed gear and rocked it forward, and then back into reverse. I slammed into the hood and put my shoulder to it as snow sprayed up from the wheels either side of me.

The pickup lurched backward and I barely caught myself before I face-planted. I turned at the sound of splintering wood and smashing glass to find . . . I don't know what to call it except a horror.

It was huge and, while most of it was covered in snow, two heads reared up from its shoulders. One was a dog, or possibly a deer – certainly it had antlers – but the other was human. He was a Caucasian male, possibly middle-aged, although it was difficult to tell. His jaw was hanging off and his eyes were white and sightless. He looked like an extra in a zombie movie, and also a good candidate to be Mr. Bunker.

I shot it in the kneecap, or at least where the kneecap should have been in the thick column of dirty white, catching the thing at the top of the stairs. The pellets blew off the snow and tore chunks off the twisted red and brown sinews beneath.

The horror staggered, caught itself. I shot it again, hoping to at least cripple it, but it regained its balance and started lurching down toward me. I backed off while chambering another shell, and it was then I realised that the engine roar from Walker's pickup was getting farther away.

I looked over my shoulder in time to see his taillights vanishing up the gap in the trees that marked the start of the driveway.

'You goddamn son of a bitch!' I screamed after him, and got the fudge out of there.

12

I like to think that I maintain a higher standard of fitness than mandated by the Bureau. I run every day, hit the gym three times a week and eat a sensible meal at least once every three days. But running in a foot of snow is its own kind of agony. That nightmare where you're running in one place – that's what it's like. The only thing worse than that is wading through waist-high sewage – that's a true comparison, by the way.

I tried to stick to the tracks of Scott Judas Iscariot Walker's pickup. That was probably the gravelled driveway, which at least didn't have any garden features hidden under the snow. Once I was a hundred yards away I risked a look back.

The garden lights might have been off but luckily the exterior lights around the entrance were still on. I could see the big horror limping toward me as a lurching silhouette. Behind it came more man-shaped things. But, worryingly, scampering ahead were small creatures running on four or more legs.

The man-shaped horrors were not fast, but the dog things scrambled through the snow swiftly enough to create a bow wave. I turned and pushed on, feeling the sweat trickling treacherously down my back and the strain settling into my thighs and butt. High stepping is not sustainable over the long run, and I certainly wasn't going to stop until I had a defensible position. At the very least.

The woods adjoining the hotel grounds were old growth, mature white pine and other conifers. A thick enough canopy to thin out the snow on the ground.

I got off the driveway on the basis that broken ground with little snow was better than tarmac with plenty. It was noticeably warmer among the trees, and the air I was sucking in no longer burned the back of my throat. There was also a noticeable slope – the start of Eloise Point, I remembered. I headed up on the assumption that having the high ground was always useful.

After two hundred yards or so I turned to check the pursuit. There was just enough light to make out the driveway as a pale line through the trees. Darker shadows moved along the road, pacing laboriously. I made out the heavy tread of the two-headed horror, and what looked like men dragging themselves through the snow.

I entertained the hope that I wasn't their quarry and instead they would continue chasing after the others. Preferably focusing on the treacherous dirtbag Walker, rather than Mrs Cole or Ashley.

Either way, they were in a working vehicle and would have reached Eloise proper by now. I hoped they had the sense to shelter with Deputy Larson and her table full of neatly stacked shotguns.

There was a flare of orange light from the direction of the hotel, and a moment later the low *whumpf* sound of a gas explosion. There must have been a fire in the kitchen or by the generator in the basement. My money was on gasoline. Propane tanks are built sturdy and you really have to mess with them to get a bang.

The light threading through the trees illuminated dirty shapes stumbling and crawling up the slope toward me.

I started upslope, but it got so dark I had to risk using my backup flashlight to pick out a path. Behind me, I could hear thumps and crashes and breaking twigs. I hoped that meant the dog things weren't coping with the darkness any better than I was.

And the noises behind me were getting closer. The creatures were gaining on me.

I was panting again, and the blood was thumping in my ears. My focus was narrowed down to the cone of light from my flashlight as it jumped about among the dark vertical shapes of the trees and the shadowy tangles of rocks and undergrowth. I was playing a weird game in which I tried to calculate each step precisely, to cover each yard in the most efficient manner possible.

The dog things were getting closer, and I started to pray.

Nothing coherent – just a wordless appeal to Jesus for a bit of assistance in my hour of need.

I was so focused on both tasks that I didn't notice I'd reached a road until I had stumbled halfway across it. It was sliced into the hillside, so that a wall of cut stone blocked my route up the hill. But I was just about fine with that, since I was panting for breath and my legs were aching. At least with something solid at my back I wouldn't have to worry about being surprised.

It turned out I was wrong, but not in the way you're thinking.

I had the flashlight in my left hand clamped up against the pump-action. It was awkward, but at least I'd be able to see what I was shooting at. I put my back against the wall of the cut, let my breathing slow and waited for the first target.

It seemed like it took a surprisingly long time.

Then one of the dog things came scrambling out of the treeline and straight at me.

I waited for it to get close and then shot it just where, in a real animal, its neck joined its chest. Snow and chunks of pulpy black and red stuff blew out of its chest. The front legs folded up and it collapsed almost at my feet.

It twitched, but I held my fire. I only had three shells left and I didn't want to waste a shot.

I shifted to my left as the thing at my feet shuddered, a quiver running down the length of its body, and then slumped. Its snow covering collapsed and lost its shape. I poked it with my foot, and what might have been its head rolled away.

They're not indestructible, I thought. *That's encouraging.*

Another 'thing' came shambling out of the treeline. Either it had been created wrong, or it had lost parts of itself along the way. One leg was a stump half the length of the other three. Instead of a maw, it had a wide frog-like mouth that seemed paralysed on the left side.

It approached slowly, dragging itself through the fresh snow on the road. I let it get closer and made a near-fatal mistake. While I was focused on the first creature, a second came flying at my face, launching itself out of the woods like a bug on a griddle. It was only a miracle that I got the shotgun up in time and fired. I jumped left as the thing hit the wall of the cut and slid, spasming, down into the snow, a crater where its head ought to be.

The shambling thing at my feet tried to take advantage, but I'd kind of expected that, and I shot down into the back of its neck.

Both creatures fell apart exactly the same as the first.

I had one shell left.

My mama calls it counting your blessings, but my firearms instructor called it being tactically aware.

I had one shell left, maybe ten rounds left in my pistol, and fifteen in the spare magazine in my shoulder holster. There had been dozens, if not more, of those creatures, but they seemed less robust than the ones I'd shot in the hotel. Those had shrugged off pistol rounds and had only been mildly inconvenienced by the shotgun.

These – and I shuffled a couple of steps away from their corpses – disintegrated after one shot. Almost as if whatever unholy force was holding them together was less effective the farther away they were from . . .

From what?

Act now, speculate later.

One shell left, but I was feeling less winded . . . so time to move.

Up or down the road?

Down was where the creatures were. Up was the meteorology station, which might, I hoped, have a shelter

– maybe a defensible one. For added optimism, Boyd might still be up there with his tricked-out pickup.

I want to state for the record that I was planning to go up even before the next wave of horrors came staggering up the road toward me. I turned to run again when I was blinded by the headlamps of an oncoming vehicle.

I could see nothing, but I could hear a vehicle suddenly skidding in the snow as the driver stood on the brakes. I threw myself out of the way and slammed into the cold wall of the cut, and turned in time to see Boyd's pickup slide past.

There was a meaty *thunk* sound as it hit the lead creature, and the truck halted just past my position. I didn't waste time trying to get in the cab. Instead I half-vaulted, half-rolled into the flatbed. Then I clambered over the equipment in the back – less than there had been before – and banged on the roof, shouting 'Go, go, go!'

Caught in his headlamps was a mass of squirming, staggering horrors. One that looked like a monkey made out of bits of squirrel and wrapped in snow had jumped on to the hood. I used the last shell on it, dropped the shotgun while the thing was still falling to bits, and pulled my pistol.

The shot must have woken Boyd up, because the engine roared, the wheels spun and we started hurtling backward. I'd been expecting Boyd to drive forward – to use the pickup to plough its way through the creatures.

I mean, what are bull bars for, if not to clear the roads of snow zombies?

Also, driving backward at speed up a twisting narrow hill road with no guardrails, in heavy snow, was insane.

I was tempted to throw myself off the pickup and take my chances with the monsters.

We turned a corner in the road and kept on turning until I realised we were backing into a wide spot cut into the hill. I caught a glimpse of a sign but I didn't have time to read past SCENIC VIEW . . . before Boyd wrenched the wheel around and roared up the road again. Going in the right direction – Lord be praised.

It went suddenly dark, and moisture beaded on my hair and face. The beams of the headlamps were shredded by fog and I realised we were in the clouds. Visibility was less than five yards, and I might have been terrified at the speed with which Boyd drove if I hadn't already been in all-out terror at that point.

And then we were out under a clear night sky, and the road flattened out and Boyd stopped and made another, much slower, three-point turn. We were at the top of Eloise Point beneath the cold glittering stars, and I found I was panting with relief.

Boyd leaned out of the cab and swung a flashlight around until he found me.

'Are you OK?' he asked.

'No,' I said. 'Not really.'

13

The summit of Eloise Point was, in point of fact, another hundred feet above where we were parked. The weather station itself was a pretty disappointing metal box on stilts, with a weathervane sticking up on a pole. It sat on a small plateau large enough for a truck to turn around and head back down the hill. If I'd been looking for shelter on foot, I'd have been sorely disappointed.

Boyd's cab, on the other hand, seemed overheated, and as soon as I climbed in my ears and face began to tingle, then prickle and then painfully burn. Boyd made me turn my head from side to side while he checked for frostnip. I'd done the whole run from hotel to road, and then the wild ride up the hill, with my hood down and never even noticed.

I was suddenly acutely aware of Boyd's nearness, his smell – which, given it was mostly wet clothes and sweat, shouldn't have been as nearly so attractive as it was.

Is this really the time and place? I thought. *The spirit is trying to concentrate but the flesh is weak.*

'You're going to be fine,' he said. 'Keep your face covered next time.'

'I was a little preoccupied,' I said.

'I'm going to make you some soup,' he said, and opened the driver's door.

'Aren't you going to ask me what happened?' I asked.

'First I'm going to feed you soup,' he said, climbing out. 'You're in shock.' He closed the door. 'Then we'll talk.'

I held up my hand – it was trembling.

Every day, Lord, you teach us a new lesson.

Boyd had left the engine idling and the headlamps on. Their beams pointed down the access road, so I was reasonably certain of some warning should the creatures have followed us up. To be on the safe side, I swapped out my half-empty magazine for the full one, chambered a round, and then laid my pistol in the cup holder beside me. That way I could zip up my parka and sit on my hands. In the rear-view mirror I kept an eye on Boyd as he opened the tailgate and set up a portable stove on the truck bed.

I tried to stay eyes forward and keep watch on the road.

Now that I had secured my own position, I had to pass warnings on. My hands were still shaky and worry-ingly stiff as I fished out my cell phone and was amazed to find I had an actual bar.

Chief Santire's number went straight to voicemail, so I tried Deputy Larson instead. She picked up on the second ring.

'Is Billy Bear with you?' she asked, before I could get a word in edgewise.

I said that William was with me, and we were both safe and at the top of Eloise Point. Before she could ask why I was up there, I asked whether the chief or any of his deputies were available. But she told me they were still out co-ordinating relief efforts.

I asked her to pass on warnings of . . . and there I stalled, trying to think of what to classify them as.

'Dangerous animals,' I said, and then, with a little prayer for forgiveness, 'Boyd thinks they've been driven mad by the freak weather and could be extremely dangerous. You and the chief need to be careful.'

'What type of animals?' asked Larson. 'And how careful?'

'I'm a city girl,' I lied. 'They looked like dogs, or maybe moose or deer. In any case, they attacked us on sight so you might want to grab your shotgun.'

'Oh,' she said in a suddenly small voice.

'And make sure you have plenty of shells,' I said.

'OK.' It was barely a whisper.

'There is something else you might be able to help me with,' I said.

'Sure,' she said, her voice regaining a bit of pep. I just bet Larson was the one the sheriff sent out to solve neighbour disputes and talk down drunks.

'Have you heard from Scott Walker or Mrs Cole?' I asked.

They'd called to report a catastrophic fire at the hotel and say that the road was blocked by an avalanche off Eloise Point. A clever move by Walker to stop the chief blundering into those creatures. Mrs Cole and Ashley had gone to stay with Mrs Cole's sister, who had a place on Allouez Avenue. Larson didn't know where Walker had got to.

Having followed up the urgent tasks, I asked if

she knew about a missing person by the name of Mr. Bunker, who would have been reported missing, or possibly absconded, the previous day.

'Is this important?' she asked.

'It could be important,' I said, and hoped she didn't ask why. That he might have stirred up a malignant Native American spirit was not an argument I wanted to use. Fortunately the mystique of the FBI won out, and Deputy Larson said she remembered the case.

'Chief Santire was salty on account of the tornado having wrecked the fella's pickup,' she said. 'See, it was found down by the marina, and they had only moved it to the impound spot next to the town hall the day before. The chief said it was terrible luck because once we'd impounded it, we were liable for any damage.' She made a little hiccuping laugh sound. 'Which is kind of funny, considering the amount of damage it did everywhere else.'

Larson didn't know whether Chief Santire or any of his complement of four deputies had had a chance to look into Mr. Bunker's affairs further, and all the records had been destroyed along with the town hall. Larson promised to see what she could find out when the chief got back to the emergency HQ. I asked whether any backup had arrived, but the routes at both ends of town were still impassable.

After I'd hung up I called Agent Doughty, who confirmed that road access to Eloise was currently impossible and, worse, the lake had frozen enough to block boats. What's more, the park rangers wouldn't vouch for the safety of anyone trying to drive over the ice.

Plus, the weather had been judged too severe to risk a helicopter flight.

He offered to make the attempt over the ice in any case, but I warned him off.

'We're bringing in a dogsled and team, but they can't get here until tomorrow,' he said.

I was impressed – I hadn't even thought of a dog team.

I passed on what I had about the mysterious Mr. Bunker, and confirmed that we were definitely dealing with a UC incident, but I hadn't discovered what kind yet. I briefed him about the snow monsters – that they were hard targets and that he should avoid getting too close.

He took the news grimly and far more matter-of-factly than I'm sure I would have.

'Are you sure you don't want me to attempt the ice road?' he said.

'No,' I said. 'I'm going to shelter in place at Eloise Point until sunrise and I can see what I'm doing.'

I signed off just as Boyd came back with a grande-sized travel mug filled with vegetable soup.

'I'm going to take some measurements,' he said. 'Will you be all right?'

'Be careful,' I said. 'Those things might come up the side of the hill.'

'Yeah,' he said, dragging it out. 'We need to talk about that when I'm done.'

'Of course,' I said, although I wasn't sure what I was going to say.

The soup tasted amazing, and I sat there letting the

mug warm my hands and the soup warm my insides. My pa had been a very practical man and did all the fixing around our house, including the electrics and our perpetually cranky furnace. He never panicked in a crisis. He would just divide up what needed to be done into separate jobs, rank them in order and get on with it.

I think he would have liked Boyd.

So would Mama if she got to see him in action.

I drank the soup and warmed up enough to get restless. A certain stiffness when I moved reminded me I had the folders stuffed down my sweater. So I laboriously unzipped myself and worked them out of my neckline. They were even more crumpled than before, so I opened the pickup's glove box and filed them there.

I opened Sadie Clarkson's file first, on the basis that I knew the least about her. Up until finding her file in Mr. Bunker's room, I'd assumed she was what she seemed – a librarian who'd come north looking for the small-town life.

In the New Orleans photographs, she was smartly turned out in summer dresses, or short skirts and equally short jackets in reds, yellows and blues. One of the pictures showed her sitting at a café table with a Black woman in a leather jacket and shades. On the reverse somebody had written her name, and beside it, *Who is this?* And somebody else had written *NOW*.

There were a couple of pages of printed matter. Either the writer had been incapable of writing in the crisp, clear manner I'd been trained to, or was being deliberately obtuse. The latter, I decided after reading half a page, the better to mask its content from casual snooping. To make sense of it, you had to know what some of the jargon meant, and fortunately I did.

Miss Clarkson has many contacts among the New Orleans twilight subculture.

I didn't think the author meant they were fans of a popular YA novel about vampires and werewolves – although I suppose it's possible there might be some overlap. More likely this was a reference to what the British call the demi-monde, the subculture that encompasses practitioners, the supernatural and those who are drawn to their company.

I could totally believe that New Orleans' demi-monde would be large and active.

So NOW could stand for New Orleans Witch or Wizard. It would be nice to know who she was. I'd have to ask Ms Clarkson about that.

We think the likelihood of Clarkson being a NOW or a shade or shade adjacent is high.

Shade had been confirmed by Peter Grant as a jargon term referring sometimes to a practitioner or supernatural being, although in my experience, some beings are more supernatural than others.

It is our conclusion that Clarkson was either following a lead on a CONTRAST EVENT . . .

I'd never heard of a contrast event, but the capitals suggested it was a code word. Probably related to whatever was causing deformed snowmen to run around town, kidnapping former FBI agents and terrorising blameless hoteliers.

. . . or was directed here by the NOW network.

Oh, it was a network now. A NOW network now. I could definitely feel a field trip down to New Orleans coming on. I was owed some warm weather after all this snow, anyway.

It went on to speculate that Clarkson had hooked up with local amateur historian and FBI agent Patrick Henderson, and they had started investigating the *MIKE1843 ECHO*...

I sighed. It was like reading a dossier from a Hollywood thriller; the obfuscations seemed mostly for show. MIKE1843ECHO was obviously the Marsh 1843 Expedition.

It was the opinion of whoever had compiled the dossier that the MIKE1843ECHO killsite was probably on the nearest of the uninhabited Apostle Islands, and that Henderson and Clarkson may have recovered important classified information.

I wondered what could still be considered classified information after a hundred and seventy years. The term *killsite* worried me. It had a hard militaristic sound, like something out of a war of extermination.

The Marsh expedition never came home.

Perhaps they were the ones who left their bodies at the killsite. Eaten by Walker's spirit wolves? Or something more prosaic, like an ambush by the local Native Americans. Had anyone ever asked the locals about what happened? Surely Scott Walker, ethnographer and possible magic enforcer, would have asked before now. I wondered if I should ask Boyd what he knew.

As if my thoughts had conjured him, Boyd opened the driver's door and climbed in. He'd taken time to make coffee, and offered me one of a second pair of travel mugs.

'How many sets of these do you have?' I asked.

'There can be a lot of standing around outside in meteorology,' he said, and then, looking over at the dossier, 'Is that Sadie? Are you investigating Sadie?'

'I'm worried about her safety,' I said.

'Why?' he asked, and I hesitated.

You really are not supposed to share your work product with civilians, and while I was tempted to explain, there were some loose ends I wanted tied up first.

'You haven't asked me about the monsters,' I said. 'The very first thing most people would have asked once we stopped was, "What the fudge was that?"'

'Except most people wouldn't have said "fudge".'

'Don't change the subject.'

'You were in shock,' he said. 'I figured if you had some soup and some quiet, you were more likely to give me a coherent explanation.'

'That's pretty cold-blooded,' I said, and sipped the coffee.

'So what just chased us up this hill?'

'Would you believe magical Frankenstein monsters made out of bits of animals and plants?'

I decided to leave out the human head on the big horror at the hotel.

There was a long silence from beside me and I risked a peek. Boyd's lips were pursed, and he stared out of the windshield, nodding to himself.

'OK,' he said finally. 'Magic.'

'You're taking this amazingly calmly,' I said.

'I've just put up a balloon that recorded an extremely strong temperature inversion aloft,' he said, 'and down here I'm seeing accelerating updraughts, too, which means the dense air is rising. Which is not just unlikely, but in active defiance of Archimedes' principle. Which I don't need to tell you is a very important principle us meteorologists hold dear.' He took a sip of coffee and looked at me. 'So magical creatures are not really coming as that much of a surprise. Therefore I think my next question has to be – are the two linked?'

'It seems likely,' I said, and we both sat in silence for about a minute until I broke down and asked what all the meteorology jargon meant.

'You'd better come and have a look for yourself,' he said.

14

The summit of Eloise Point, according to Boyd, was 1,078 feet above sea level, with the observation point a hundred feet below the summit and facing the lake. A waning crescent moon hung above the eastern horizon. In its pale light the frozen lake was a dim grey sheet from which islands loomed as dark shapes. Boyd pointed out a large island to the south-east whose humped darkness was sprinkled with clusters of artificial light. Unmistakably houses and roads.

'That's La Pointe on Madeline Island,' he said.

A smaller patch of darkness, much closer but without lights, was Basswood Island. Both were part of the Apostle Islands National Lakeshore.

The sky had a fantastic glittering clarity, which Boyd explained was because of the moisture that had been drawn out of it and was now currently falling as heavy snow along the coast.

'Is that normal?' I asked.

The summit proper blocked our view of Eloise, but we could see up the coastline toward Red Cliff – or at least we could have if it hadn't been obscured by a solid bank of low-level cloud.

'Not normal,' said Boyd. 'I would have said "not even

remotely possible" if I wasn't looking at it right now. And had the readings to back it up.'

On the bright side, he was pretty sure he could get a good paper out of his observations.

'Even though you say this weather wasn't possible,' I said.

'That's the joy of meteorology,' he said. 'There's vast areas of doubt and uncertainty.'

'For example?'

'Lightning,' he said. 'We don't know what causes it.'

'Yes we do.'

'No we don't.'

'Really?'

'Really.'

I was tempted to say that this showed that science didn't have an answer for everything, except I had a nagging suspicion that I might be missing the point. Certainly Boyd seemed excited about his ignorance, and it made him seem younger and, annoyingly, even more attractive.

Seriously, I thought not for the first time, *is this the time and place?*

But his enthusiasm did give me an opening.

'Do you know of any . . .' I hesitated, remembered Walker's lecture and searched for the right word . . . 'traditions that could explain this?'

'Are you asking me as a meteorologist or an Ojibwe?'

'An Ojibwe who's a meteorologist,'

'I had an uncle,' he said. 'He wasn't really my uncle by blood, but he was my uncle anyhow, if you know what I mean. He was older than my dad, and when we went back to the rez for the holidays we used to stay with him. He used to take me out for hikes and tell me stuff.'

'What kind of stuff?'

'Practical things, tracking, animals, trees – he liked trees,' he said. 'Stories.'

'What kind of stories?'

'Kids' stories – how the raccoon got its mask, how the birch tree got its stripes. Stories about Nanaboozhoo and his many tricks and gifts.'

'Nanabushzoo?'

'Nanaboozhoo,' said Boyd. '*Boozhu*, not *booshu*.'

'Was there anything relevant?'

'To this?' Boyd waved his hand at the moonlit ice. 'Nothing that comes to mind. Although I think perhaps I should have listened harder when I was a kid. You don't, though, do you – listen to elders when you're young.'

Nanaboozhoo, I thought.

I'd heard of trickster spirits in other mythologies. Was he the target of the 1843 expedition? Was he the devil Captain Marsh wished to eliminate?

'Could he turn into a wolf?' I asked.

'Who?'

'Nanaboozhoo.'

'He could become any animal or person,' said Boyd. 'But he didn't create an army of Frankenstein snow monsters, if that's what you're implying. At least not in any stories my uncle told me.'

Maybe he's picked up some new tricks, I thought, and shivered. The wind was rising, howling around the bald hilltop, and I was getting cold again.

'Let's go back to the truck,' I said.

Once we were back in the warmth, I showed him the pictures of Sadie Clarkson and asked what he knew about her.

'She's a librarian,' he said, and then after a pause, 'From New Orleans.'

'I think she's what we call a "practitioner",' I said. 'Someone who can do magic.'

'OK . . . magic,' said Boyd. 'Magic, magic, magic. Yes, magic.'

This is a fairly common reaction, and some people never really do reconcile themselves that magic is as real as death, taxes and political advertising. Boyd accepted it all surprisingly quickly; perhaps it was his uncle – or the snow monsters – but by the time I'd explained *vestigia* he was nodding to himself.

'You know, weirdly, that makes sense,' he said. 'And Sadie is a practitioner?'

'I think so,' I said.

'She never did anything magical in front of me,' said Boyd. 'Except maybe she could recite the world's longest Dewey Decimal number, which was kind of cool.'

'You've never been to her house?'

'No,' he said. 'But I don't come to Eloise that often. I'm usually up at the Cliffs or down at Ashland. I only came here yesterday because of the tornado.'

'You seemed pretty friendly at the library.'

'Friendliness is a key meteorological superpower,' he said. 'You never know when Charlie Shortino might decide to retire.'

I must have looked blank because he continued,

'He's been the weather guy at NBC15 for forever.' And, after another pause, 'He's a very likeable guy. I've met him. He came and gave a talk at the college when I was a freshman.'

I switched to the dossier on Scott Walker.

'What about Walker?' I said. 'He seemed to know you.'

'I've seen him around on the rez, and also down at Bad River.' Another reservation to the south of Bayfield. 'He's like you – always asking about stories.' He tapped the dossier. 'Is this an FBI file?'

'No,' I said, and told him about Mr. Bunker, and about the third file that was about Patrick Henderson.

'And you think a vengeful Native spirit has risen up to punish the white man for his crimes against the indigenous population?' asked Boyd.

'It's a theory,' I said. 'You saw the snow monsters. What do you think?'

'I think I should have listened harder to my uncle when I had the chance,' he said. 'But this doesn't feel like something that comes from us.' He tapped his chest.

'Truthfully,' I said, 'all I have is a bag full of somebodies and somethings.'

Somebody had compiled the dossiers on Henderson, Walker and Clarkson.

'Three people who have a working knowledge of the supernatural,' I said. 'Then something came off the lake and snatched Patrick Henderson, and then came up again and went after Scott Walker.'

'How do you know Mrs Cole wasn't the target?'

Good question.

My gut said Walker had been the target, but I didn't have any evidence as such. Still, where the snow monsters went after the hotel could answer that question.

'Let's assume that Walker was a target,' I said. 'Then the question is why? Is it something about him – something he knows, or something he has?'

I thought suddenly of the silver dollar and the unmistakable *vestigium* that had clung to it.

'Oh darn,' I said.

'What?'

I told him about the silver dollar with a hole through it, the complexity of the *vestigium* and the sudden icy stab to the chest.

'Could it have been a necklace?' I asked. 'Could several dollars have been strung together.'

'All sorts of stuff gets made for tourists these days,' he said. 'But I've never seen anything like that at a ceremony or a meeting.'

'So it's not authentic?'

'That's another loaded word,' said Boyd. 'It implies there is an authentic and inauthentic Ojibwe culture that is historically fixed, rather than a living culture that is constantly evolving, just like every other culture.'

'OK,' I said. 'You understood my meaning?'

'Of course I did,' he said. 'But you could have asked me whether I thought such a necklace might have been made by an Ojibwe.'

'So do you?'

'Can't say,' he said. 'Not without an actual necklace or similar. All you have is a silver dollar with a hole in it.'

'Are you always this persnickety?'

'No,' said Boyd. 'You can get tired of correcting people all the time. These days I only do it in exceptional cases.'

'I'm honoured.'

'You should be,' said Boyd. 'I don't go all politically correct for just anyone, you know.'

'I feel special,' I said.

It might have been the soup, or the warmth of the cab, but suddenly I had a crazy urge to rest my head on Boyd's shoulder and go to sleep. Just for ten minutes, maybe twenty, or possibly an hour . . .

'Can I see it?' asked Boyd suddenly.

I jerked fully awake.

'See what?'

'The coin.'

'Ashley has it,' I said.

We turned to look at each other, and I could see in his face that he was jumping to the same conclusion I was.

Less than a minute later, we were heading down the access road with our seat belts on and my pistol in my hand.

I had one service bar on my phone, and tried Deputy Larson. She told me that Walker had checked in and said he was up at the library. He hadn't said whether Ashley or Mrs Cole were with him. I asked whether they'd encountered any strange animal activity – still the best euphemism for 'snow monster' I could come up with – but Larson said no. But on a more optimistic note, the chief was fairly certain that nobody else was missing.

Except Mr. Bunker, I thought, but he wasn't a local so probably didn't count.

I lost cell coverage as soon as we dropped into the clouds, and Boyd slowed and changed traction control as the truck started to plough through fresh snow. Trees started to flick past on the right, and then on both sides of the road as it bottomed out into the valley. We must have passed the spot where Boyd picked me up the first time, but I didn't recognise it with the snow and speed.

We encountered our first snow monsters as soon as we turned on to the highway. A scattering of misshapen figures lurching and limping up the road ahead of us.

'Blow through, blow through!' I shouted.

Boyd gunned the engine. He tried to swerve around them when he could, but he caught a thin scarecrow-like thing in the back and it disintegrated. Something head-shaped bounced off the windshield, leaving a splash of bile-green liquid that was then smeared across the glass by the wipers.

We were basically returning to the library the way we'd come, so despite the darkness, the absence of street-lamps, and the way the snow swallowed our headlamps, I recognised the turn-off up Allouez Avenue. The town's power was still out, but a couple of businesses obviously had generators. Mrs Cole's sister had her house on the avenue. I hoped for Ashley's sake that it was at this end, and far from the library. One business, Mandy's Bar and Grill, had a spotlight on the Stars and Stripes hanging proudly in the window. I caught a glimpse of patrons eating and drinking through the windows before Boyd shifted traction modes again and gunned it up the hill.

Then I felt it – a burst of heat, as if I had stepped out of a shaded door and into summer sun. With it came the rank smell of still water and the taste of strong liquor and the last note of an old sad song.

Then it was gone, so fast that I wasn't sure I'd actually felt anything at all.

But I knew what it was – another *vestigium*. Peter Grant says that the more often you recognise them, the better you become at sensing them, until they become almost a background noise, like birdsong or road traffic.

Magic had been done nearby and, if I was any judge, it had been strong magic.

I glanced at Boyd, who was concentrating on getting us up the hill without skidding.

Ahead, the library was ablaze with light, every window brightly lit and the stairs and mobility ramp illuminated with floodlights. In front, down at street level, were the blackened husks of two burned-out vehicles, one a pickup truck and the other the Toyota that I'd signed the papers for that morning.

And I hadn't even bothered to check the exception clauses on the insurance.

All the snow, from the library facade down to the street parking, was pockmarked and cratered. Small dark twisted shapes were scattered among the holes. The remains, I saw as we drew closer, of dismembered snow monsters.

The library entrance doors were missing, but the inner doors were intact.

I directed Boyd to park farther up the avenue so we could approach the library from the rear. It turned out there was a staff parking lot at the back, so we turned in to that. Boyd, without me even asking, parked his truck pointing back out of the lot.

'In case we need to leave in a hurry,' he said.

When he turned off the ignition it was suddenly very quiet.

I pulled my pistol so I could zip back up before leaving the truck. Boyd gave me a questioning look.

'Maybe you should stay in the truck,' I said.

'No,' he said. 'I think I should come and help out.'

'You don't have to.'

'Yes I do,' he said. 'It's that small-town esprit de corps.'

'You said you grew up in Madison.'

'Yeah,' he said, 'but it has that small town feel.'

I opened the door and got out.

'Stay behind me,' I said.

The rear fire exit was a steel door set in a blind stretch of brick. The pristine snow indicated that nobody had gone in or out in the last hour. I wondered why the snow monsters hadn't tried the back. Were they really that mindless? And if they were, what was directing their actions? Quietly I tried the handle, but it was locked.

I listened at the door and heard voices, so I slapped it hard with the palm of my hand.

'Open up!' I shouted, and out of sheer training reflex added, 'It's the FBI!'

I heard a familiar child's voice shout inside – Ashley.

'It's Kim, it's Kim!'

The door unlocked and was thrown open by the young girl.

'Are you here to rescue us?' she asked. 'Miss Clarkson did magic and then she fell down.'

One of my instructors at Quantico opined once that, occasionally, children can make the best witnesses, because they report what they see in the simplest way possible. The door opened directly into the children's section of the library, and Ashley was clutching a yellow and green spotted cushion to her chest.

'Where is she?' I asked.

Ashley pointed toward the front of the library.

I saw Walker with a rifle positioned to the right of the inner doors, so that he could safely peer out of their glass inserts.

Sadie Clarkson was lying on her back a couple of feet from the doors. Her face was pale but her left eye was bloodshot, the lid drooping. Her lips were moving, but I could see that the left side of her mouth was frozen. I kneeled down to hear what she was trying to say.

'Oh God,' she murmured. 'I've fucked myself.'

It looked like a stroke, but I had an inkling it was something else.

'What happened?' asked Boyd.

'Rebenstock's Syndrome,' said Walker. 'It's the reason why doing magic isn't as popular as you'd think it would be.'

He looked up at Boyd and realised that he'd slipped up.

'Don't move me,' whispered Clarkson. 'No aspirin or anti—' She winced. 'Anti-coagulants. Not a stroke.'

'Where's Mrs Cole?' I asked.

'She's gone for help,' said Walker.

'And you let her?'

I looked back at where Boyd was gently leading Ashley back to the children's section.

'It's not after her,' he said flatly.

'What isn't after her?'

'The two-headed thing,' he said. 'It's after me – I think.'

'And me,' whispered Clarkson.

'Do you know what it is?' I asked her.

'Bad spirit,' she said. 'Angry.'

'How do we stop it?'

A single tear started from her unaffected left eye.

'Don't know . . .' Her voice was dying away. 'Wanted to be friends . . .'

Her eyes closed, but while her breathing was laboured, it remained steady.

I joined Walker by the door and looked out at the pockmarked snow, the bits of animal bodies and the smouldering vehicles. I would have liked to take him to task for abandoning me to my fate back at the hotel, but I didn't have time for that.

Yet.

'What did this?' I asked.

'Sadie did,' he said. 'Some kind of area of effect spell. Never seen anything like it.'

'She said she wanted to be friends.'

'She tried, but it had other ideas, so . . .' He indicated the ruined approach to the library with the barrel of his rifle. 'She did that.'

'I thought Mrs Cole and Ashley were going to her sister's,' I said.

'They were right behind us going up Jefferson Avenue and I didn't want to drag them over toward population,' he said. 'I thought I'd lost them, so I raced up here to warn Sadie, and the next thing we knew they were on top of us again.'

'Why, though?' I said. 'Why you?'

'I don't know,' he said. 'Just lucky, I guess.'

I thought this might be an opportune moment to ask about why he'd left me to die, but before I could, Walker stiffened.

'Shit,' he said. 'It's back.'

15

I t was old Two Heads, the big snow monster from the hotel with one dead human head and one deer head, complete with antlers. Its snow covering had been torn away over great sections of torso, revealing pulsing tangles of tree roots and animal guts.

It was advancing slowly and laboriously up the disabled access ramp. Its movements were much less fluid and assured than it had been when it chased me. I got the strong impression that just moving was costing it a great deal of effort.

'Give me the rifle,' I said to Walker.

He frowned and clutched the gun tighter.

'Give me the goddamn rifle, Walker!' I shouted, and he handed it over.

It was a classic Remington 700, like the gun my Pa used to hunt with. It had a box magazine, which was good, but no scope. That was all right; I didn't think I was going to be engaging at range. I checked the breech and the safety – it was ready to go.

'You got reloads?' I asked, and Walker nodded.

I shouldered my way through the inner doors and stepped out onto the freezing concrete platform at the top of the stairs. Two Heads hesitated a moment and then, as if recognising me, lumbered into a run. Straight at me.

I haven't hunted since my dad passed and, truth be told, I was never that accurate with a rifle. Still, at ten feet it's hard to miss – even with iron sights. Remembering the dog thing I'd shot up on Eloise Point, I aimed at the pulpy mass at the top of the chest.

I don't know what Walker had loaded his rounds with, but the kick was much harder than I remembered. Snow, pulp and green ichor spurted from the left shoulder. I worked the bolt and adjusted to the right. This time I hit dead centre, and while the wound on its front was neat and round, I saw a spray of green and red behind it.

Two Heads stopped.

I worked the bolt, click-clack, and fired even as the creature turned, my shot leaving a vivid green furrow across its shoulder. Then it flung itself forward and, like a kid on a plastic tray, slid down the slope on its front.

I ran forward in time to see it climb to its feet and start lumbering across the road.

Not mindless, then, I thought. And put another round in its back. *The others attacked until they died, but this one has a sense of self-preservation.*

Sadie Clarkson had called it a bad spirit. If Two Heads was that spirit, then deal with that and you've dealt with the whole problem.

I turned back to see Boyd and Walker staring at me from the open doorway.

'Boyd,' I shouted, 'get the truck and follow me down!'

Even as I scrambled down the steps to the road, a

little voice in my head pointed out this was an amazingly stupid move.

But solve Two Heads, solve everything else.

Once I was on the road, I could hear Two Heads crashing through the undergrowth on the empty lot opposite. I high-stepped through the snow and found myself wishing for Boyd's snowshoes or, even better, skis.

By the sound of it, he was going left toward Allouez Avenue, so I trotted as fast as the snow permitted to the crossing and waited there. Despite the snow, visibility was improving and I could see the business premises at the bottom as shadowy rectangles. A warm glow of light marked Mandy's Bar and Grill and the other businesses with generators.

The marina and the lake beyond were all but invisible, but I felt them as an absence. A place where the world came to a stop.

Two Heads crashed out of the empty lot twenty feet down the hill. I was careful lining up the rifle. A long gun like that can shoot right through a person, and on through the wall of a house and an innocent party inside. The roads looked clear, so I risked putting a round in the creature's back. It shuddered with the impact and turned just in time to get a second round in the lower torso.

It might have been my imagination, but I could swear that there was something almost reproachful about the way it faced me. As if it couldn't understand why I was inflicting such damage upon its body.

Wanted to be friends, Sadie Clarkson had said.

143

I raised the rifle to my shoulder again.

The world around me was suddenly brilliant with light. Two Heads flinched back, the pulpy wounds in its torso a vivid glistening pink, yellow and green. Boyd's pickup came to a halt beside me with an alarming skid.

And while I was distracted with that, Two Heads turned and did the body surfing trick down the steep slope of the avenue.

I shouted 'Follow that thing!' at Boyd and climbed into the bed of the truck. I'd noticed a spotlight mounted on the roof bar and, putting the rifle between my knees, I held on to the bar with my left hand and fumbled for the on switch with my right. Pa would not have been happy about the gun safety, but without my grip on the bar Boyd's sudden acceleration would have put me on my backside.

The spotlight was insanely bright, and even with the snow and the mist I could easily pick out Two Heads as it bodysurfed down the middle of the avenue. I heard Boyd cursing as the truck slewed left and started sliding, forcing him to ease off to maintain control. This suited me fine; I didn't want to catch Two Heads until it was safely away from any population.

Pinned in the spotlight, Two Heads ran out of steep hill and had to lurch to its feet. As it lumbered past Mandy's Bar and Grill, I saw customers scrambling out onto the sidewalk to watch it pass. They had their phones out, and I wondered how long it would be before I would be watching blurred shots of Two Heads running past, followed by myself and Mr. William Boyd in his tricked-out Raptor.

The land flattened and we reached the marina. To the right was the remains of the town hall, and beyond that the portable floodlights that marked the temporary emergency centre where, hopefully, Deputy Larson was holding down the fort.

Straight ahead, the avenue transformed into a long concrete pier that pushed out into the lake. To the left were ranks of masts and funnels – the working boats and pleasure craft frozen into their winter berths.

Two Heads kept stomping up the pier, but Boyd turned to the right on to a gentle slipway and past a sign that said CAUTION ICE ROAD CLOSED. Then we were out onto the ice. Agent Doughty had reported that the ice hadn't been declared thick enough for traffic, but I was hoping that Boyd, being a meteorologist, knew what he was doing.

I swivelled the spotlight to keep Two Heads illuminated, and for a hundred yards we were running parallel until the creature reached the end of the pier and jumped off onto the ice. It started angling away, but Boyd turned the truck to follow.

The going across the ice was rough, but I risked leaning over and rapping on the window behind Boyd. When he wound his window down I told him to keep his distance.

'We need to know where it's going!' I shouted.

He nodded and slowed the truck.

I checked behind, but there was only a faint glow to mark where Bayfield might have been.

Two Heads continued its lumbering run ahead of us.

Now the adrenaline rush had worn off, I realised my

face was freezing again. I pulled up my scarf to cover my nose and mouth and wished I'd thought to bring snow goggles.

Next trip to the north, I thought, *for certain. A bit of follow-up at Red Cliffs.*

But even as I was distracted by the thought, Two Heads vanished.

I panned the spotlight left to right, but there was nothing but the insistent snow falling through the beam. Boyd instinctively slowed to a crawl and, looking back, probably helped save our lives.

I got a sudden sense of something moving beneath the ice. Something swift and huge. There was the shimmering crack of ice breaking, then shattering, and a thing as gnarled as a tree root and as sinuous as the tentacle of an octopus reared up into the light.

It slammed down on the roof of the cab before sliding with a rasping noise back down to the hood. I felt Boyd gun the engine, but then my stomach lurched as the truck dropped at least a foot. Then it tilted forward, and my spotlight caught on a crater in the ice a full ten yards across, with snow piled up around the edge. At the bottom was the black sheen of open water from which the tentacle had emerged. Even while I was gaping, a second tentacle flailed out to smash down on the hood.

The wheels spun and the truck jerked backward a few inches before suddenly and sickeningly tilting down. Now the front wheels were churning slush at the edge of the crater, and sprays of water flew up on either side.

I saw that the tentacles were trying to grab hold of the truck, but lacked the dexterity or anything like the hooks or suction cups that a real octopus or squid would have. Thank the Lord for small mercies. Otherwise we'd have been dragged down already.

Boyd was still trying to reverse out, but I could see it wasn't going to happen. The rear wheels had lifted off the ground and the front were churning water. I banged on the roof of the cab and shouted to Boyd that it was time to leave. I didn't wait to see if he'd heard me, and vaulted over the side into the snow.

The truck tilted forward again and I dove forward to wrench open the driver's door. To my horror, instead of jumping out, Boyd twisted in his seat and, leaning over the backrest, started groping around for something.

I felt a pulse of something angry and unmistakably malignant. The truck lurched and, with a high-pitched grinding noise, started sinking through the ice.

Time's up, I thought, and grabbed Boyd's parka and threw myself away from the truck. I heard Boyd yelling in surprise as I yanked him out of the cab. He landed on top of my chest, winding me but quickly rolling off. I think I heard him say sorry.

There was a splintering sound and I scrambled backward through the snow. The light in the cab flickered out and it was suddenly pitch black.

Another pulse of angry contempt and a gurgling, drowning sound.

I felt Boyd grab my arm and drag me away.

There was a final *gloop*, and then nothing but a faint sound as the water in the crater sloshed against its sides.

16

I got to my feet and fumbled my flashlight out of my pocket. A bright light swept over me as Boyd did the same. I pointed my light back at where the truck had been, but it was gone. There was nothing left except a ragged crater in the ice. Fresh transparent ice was starting to form on the lake water at the bottom of the crater, the surface sheen reflecting the beam of my flashlight.

Low cloud blacked out the sky and heavy snow brought the visibility, even with a light, down to less than ten feet, big snowflakes falling remorselessly down through the beam.

'My truck!' shouted Boyd in almost a wail, and then in a more normal, serious voice, 'The FBI's going to pay for that, right?'

'Hopefully,' I said, although the Bureau really hates paying out for anything – even lunch expenses.

'Did any part of you go in the water?' asked Boyd.

I checked myself and found that all my inner layers were dry. I told him no and he sighed with relief. I saw he was clutching a white canvas body bag, which he slung over his shoulder. It was what he'd been groping for when I'd pulled him out of the cab. I hoped it was full of survival gear, but it looked half-empty to me.

I thought of the tentacles that had come writhing out of the hole.

'We should move away from here,' I said.

'Any idea of what direction?' asked Boyd.

My cell phone had a GPS-enabled compass app, but when I fumbled it out of my jacket pocket, the screen was blank and it made a rainmaker sound when I shook it by my ear. Boyd's was the same, so we were effectively lost.

'I had a proper compass in the truck,' said Boyd.

'Away,' I said. 'I think the important direction is away.'

Boyd insisted on taking point, and I walked behind him with my fingers curled around the bag strap across his back. Less snow had fallen out on the lake, but even with Boyd breaking the way ahead of me, walking was hard work. I kept my head down and concentrated on putting one foot in front of the other.

According to Peter Grant, there had been two founding schools of magic in the United States, each based on the European magical tradition codified by Sir Isaac Newton. One, unsurprisingly, formed by Benjamin Franklin and based at the university he himself had founded in Philadelphia. The other by Thomas Jefferson and based in Charlottesville, Virginia, where his own university was founded. Given their founders, it was hardly surprising that the two magic schools were rivals, or that they ended up on opposite sides in the Civil War.

The militant wing of the Jeffersonian wizards was the Virginian Gentlemen's Company, and it was practitioners from Virginia who led the Marsh expedition to the

Great Lakes region in 1843. Their purpose – to eliminate a troublesome Native 'devil' that had plagued European settlement in what was then the Wisconsin Territory.

Trapped by the lake icing over – I laughed to myself at that point – they went into winter camp north of Eloise Point, about where Mrs Cole's hotel was now. On the south side of the point was a Native village. A young man, supposedly from this village, approached Marsh in his camp and offered to guide him to where the 'devil' lived.

Marsh assembles his men and they head off across the ice, never to be seen again.

Wherever they ended up, they either died of exposure or some such natural misadventure, or were eaten by shapeshifting wolves.

As I plodded in a weird dissociated state behind Boyd, I decided that the former was more plausible. Especially since I might be on the verge of a practical demonstration of how easy it was to die of exposure in an unforgiving northern winter.

But the arrival of the snow monsters, particularly Two Heads, and whatever horrible thing had just tried to drag us under the ice, suggested that their fate may have been a bit more supernatural than mere exposure.

Had something woken up that 'devil'?

Cymbeline had said that nature spirits were springing up all over. Could this include a spirit with an ancient grudge against the people who had tried to hunt it down? In which case, what exactly did it want and, more importantly, how could I stop it?

Boyd himself now stopped so suddenly I nearly ran into his back.

'We need to shelter in place,' he said.

'There's nothing here,' I said. 'We'll freeze.'

'We might not,' he said. 'I have a secret weapon.'

'Wait! Might not?'

'We'll have a better chance than if we keep walking.'

He bent down and started pawing at the snow – piling it up.

'A snow cave?' I asked.

'Too dangerous, wrong conditions. But snow is a better insulator than ice.'

Once I saw he was making a platform, I crouched down and helped, although he told me not to overexert.

'We don't want to get sweaty,' he said.

He unslung the cross bag from his shoulder and, reaching in. pulled out a rolled-up red and white checked cloth. He thrust it into my hands and I realised it was the type of blanket you'd lay down for a picnic.

'This is your survival bag?' I asked.

Boyd pulled a puffy silver rectangle from the bag, unzipped one side, unfolded it and laid it down on the snow. I realised it was a collapsible cool box. He traded the bag for the blanket and, draping that over his shoulders, sat down on the insulated fabric of the cool box. He spread his legs.

'Are you sitting down or no?' he asked.

I sat down between his legs, where he'd left enough insulation to stop my backside from immediately freezing. He then swept the blanket up and around until we were covered from the tops of our heads to our legs. Or rather, we were covered on the third attempt.

'It's not so easy with two people,' he said.

It kept some of the wind off, but I could still feel the heat being sucked away.

'So now we freeze in the dark?' I said.

He laughed softly. I felt his breath on my cheek.

'We haven't deployed the secret weapon yet,' he said. 'Open the bag for me.'

I held the canvas bag open and he reached around to grope inside it.

'Aha,' he said and pulled something out – it was a tea-light, a larger version of the things I bought from Ikea.

I felt him reach around with his left hand – there was a rasping sound and then a flame. He had a Bic disposable lighter in his hand, which he used to light the tealight in his right. The wick on the stumpy candle flickered and then burned steadily.

'It is better to light a candle,' he said, 'and input additional calories into a confined space, than to curse the darkness. Between the two of us and this candle, we should be able to keep warm until sunrise.'

'Are there any other surprises in the bag?'

'I don't know,' he said. 'I came up north in a hurry and didn't think to restock it. Have a look.'

He held the tea light while I had a rummage, and came up with some plastic clothes pegs that we used to fasten the blanket so it wouldn't blow open. There was a deformed seven-ounce Hershey bar at the bottom, which we sniffed dubiously as we debated whether chocolate could go dangerously rotten or not. We each tried a square and decided it was worth taking a risk.

After chocolate we shifted position. I shuffled back until my back was pressed firmly against Boyd's chest. We were, I figured, going to need all the heat we could keep.

More heat than I'd anticipated when I felt an unfamiliar flush starting in my stomach and between my legs. Unfamiliar, because it had been a while since I'd met a man who provoked me that way, let alone snuggled up against one for warmth. He smelled of wet waterproof, sweat and chocolate, and I was conscious suddenly that I hadn't had a shower since Washington. Not that that seemed to matter to the hot feeling in my chest, back and face.

I had boyfriends in high school, despite Mama being a firm believer in abstinence and saving yourself for marriage. I've had lovers. Heck, I've even taken a couple home to meet my mama, who was polite enough at dinner, although there was no question of them sharing my bedroom overnight.

When I was a teen, my mama used to fret that I might marry somebody other than a right-thinking evangelical Christian man, preferably from the Midwest. Recently she's made it clear that she'll accept any flavour of Christian other than Mormon. I suspect that in a few years she'll be willing to accept anyone who was raised in the Abrahamic tradition, providing they're an American citizen.

My younger brother, who lives on the next block over from my mama's house, is a lay preacher and has three children, says that I should take home a nice Christian woman as an experiment. In fact, he offered to pay her airfare just so he could watch the result.

The truth is that recently there'd been a marked short-age of men in my life who made me consider buying frilly underwear. And I wasn't about to get out of bed, or even back in, for anything less.

But now there were no two ways about it. I was hot and bothered over Mr. William Boyd and I hadn't even asked whether he was a practising Christian yet. I turned my face toward his and saw his lips twitch up. I knew it was mutual from the look in his eyes, so I kissed him, because I'd just been reminded that life is short.

He kissed me back and I felt his arms tighten around me.

There was no chance of it going any further. Neither of us were about to unzip anything, let alone shed any items of clothing. So we ended up making out like a pair of repressed teenagers at the old Beacon Drive-in in Guthrie.

We paused after a while and just sat together with our cheeks touching and the ice melting off the fur around my hood. I think we dozed for a bit, because when I opened my eyes the candle had burned down until it guttered in its foil container.

A young voice called from outside.

'Hello, is anyone still alive in there?'

17

I considered pulling my pistol, but that seemed a bit of an overreaction. I then considered jumping up and rolling to the left, but my legs were stiff. And judging by the weight against our blanket, snow had piled up around us. I decided that if I wasn't going to be sudden and impulsive, I might as well be slow and methodical. I signalled to Boyd to stay quiet, pinched out the last bite of flame on the tealight and unclipped the front of the blanket. Brilliant white sunlight flooded in.

A teenaged boy stood a nice respectful six feet away. He was dressed in fake camouflage cargo pants and a blue puffer jacket. The hood was thrown back to reveal a beautiful oval face with elegant cheekbones, a strong patrician nose over an expressive mouth, and dark intelligent eyes. His complexion was darker than Boyd's but I could see the kinship.

'A pair of snowbirds,' he said as Boyd and I climbed stiffly to our feet.

I looked around and saw we were less than a couple of hundred yards from the shoreline – ruddy sandstone cliffs with snow-covered woods rising behind. Given the position of the sun in the east, this must be one of the

Apostle Islands. When I looked west, the lake shore was hidden by a slate-coloured bank of cloud.

'Hi,' he said, and then looked over at Boyd and spoke a few words in a language I couldn't identify.

Boyd answered back in kind, although he stumbled over a couple of words.

The boy inclined his head.

'You guys want to get out of this weather?' he said. 'My cabin's just over there.'

We shook out the blanket, folded it and the portable cooler, and stowed them in the bag. Something about the way the boy looked at us made me make sure the remains of the tealight, the pegs, and even the Hershey wrapper were collected and taken with us.

'My name is Kimberley,' I said. 'What's yours?'

'I haven't decided yet,' he said, and headed off toward the island.

'I can't believe we were this close to the island,' I said to Boyd as we followed the boy.

'You were going in the wrong direction,' said the boy, without looking back.

'He's right,' said Boyd. 'We sheltered facing the way we came. If we'd carried on we'd be out there somewhere.'

He pointed out to where the lake ice merged into the morning haze.

There was something odd about the way the boy walked across the snow. It was deep, and Boyd and I had to take high steps to make progress. The boy didn't seem to have this problem – as if he were stepping so lightly that his feet didn't sink all the way in.

I'd met some strange people in London, not even

counting the ones who could do magic. The boy was definitely *something*, and I wondered whether it was worth asking him what.

But not just then. Teenage make-out session or not, we weren't that well rested. And walking through the snow left me with little breath to ask difficult questions. Or even easy ones like, 'Are we there yet?'

We came off the ice in a cove that was like a neat circular bite out of the sandstone cliffs. A flight of concrete steps twisted up the ten feet or so to the top, and we emerged into a clearing. An honest-to-God log cabin sprawled in the middle of it. It had obviously started as a simple rectangular building on a stone foundation, but had grown a porch, additional rooms, a side porch and lean-tos for storing firewood and a snowmobile. A large satellite dish sat incongruously on the woodshed. There was no sign of a car or a pickup or, I realised, anything that resembled a road or path wide enough to drive down.

A man was chopping wood in front of the porch, methodically working his way through a pile of logs. He'd stripped down to his red checked flannel shirt for the work, showing a heavily developed chest and shoulders.

Jail or time in the Marines, I thought, although both were possible.

His hair was long and dirty brown, drawn back into a ponytail. He looked up as we approached and I saw narrow grey eyes over a broken nose and a thin mouth. He looked two weeks short of his last shave.

He kept the axe in his hands as we approached.

159

'Look what I found in the snow,' said the boy as we approached.

The man's shoulders relaxed some, but his grip on the axe did not.

'This is Travis,' said the boy by way of introduction, although he didn't slow down and we felt compelled to follow him past the man and his axe. He nodded in my direction.

'Ma'am,' he said.

'Kimberley,' I said, which was a breach of FBI protocol.

'*Aanii*,' he said to Boyd, who responded.

'Bill,' said Boyd – which was a mistake, because now he was going to be Bill to me forever.

'They're going to need blankets,' said the boy, without turning to look back.

We shed our coats and boots in the porch and the cold chased us inside, nipping at our toes.

The interior of the log cabin was surprisingly modern, fitted out like the lakeside retreat of a prosperous dentist. Polished wooden floorboards strewn with rugs, a kitchen corner with a table big enough to eat at, double-glazed windows, a fieldstone fireplace with a couch and easy chairs arranged to catch the glow. There weren't any stuffed animal heads or antlers mounted on the walls, but instead the sort of Native American style woven wall hangings that they sell in souvenir shops and on Etsy. There were doors leading off the main room, and through one came Travis with blankets.

The boy had offered to run all our clothes through their washer-dryer, and ushered me into his room to change. Apart from the wall hangings and the fact that the bed was neatly made, it could have been any teen boy's room. There was a poster from *Spirited Away* and another Japanese animated film I didn't recognise. A laptop, school binders and what proved to be middle school textbooks.

I considered leaving on my bra and undies, but I'd been wearing them continuously for over a day. So I wrapped a pretty tan and salmon-pink blanket around my waist as a long skirt and found that Travis had donated me one of his T-shirts. I assumed it belonged to Travis, because it fit me like a tent and I had to roll the sleeves up. I threw another patterned cotton blanket, this one with olive and lilac flowers on a black background, over my shoulders. In the absence of any complimentary slippers, I left my socks on. Travis knocked on the door, and when I said I was decent, he came in and collected my clothes. He checked the washing labels on my thermals and grunted before whisking them away toward the back of the cabin.

I caught the buttered toast smell of fresh trout being fried, and when I entered the main room I saw the boy was shaking a frying pan over the burner. He turned away long enough to smile and point me at the kitchen table, which had been set for breakfast.

I was so hungry that my mouth actually watered and my stomach rumbled. There was a bowl of wild rice topped with toasted pecans and maple syrup. Contrary to the way I was raised, I stirred in the maple syrup and started immediately, although to keep Mama happy I tried to take small, ladylike spoonfuls. She used to say that a proper appetite was the best sauce for any meal, which might explain why that was the tastiest bowl of rice I've ever had. Not that I eat rice for breakfast normally, and definitely not sweetened with maple syrup.

Bill came in, looking good in a blanket sarong and a faded blue T-shirt that fit him much better than mine did me.

'Morning,' he said, and sat down next to me. He glanced down at his rice and then up at the boy with a wry smile.

'You're laying it on a bit thick, aren't you?' he said.

'There's Cheerios in the cupboard if you prefer,' said the boy, grinning.

'I'm good,' said Bill, and started eating.

We were both too busy eating to talk, although I wanted to ask the boy his name again, but it didn't seem like an appropriate moment. We'd barely finished our rice when the boy presented us with plates of fried trout fillets, squash and potato. Then he fetched himself a glass of milk and sat down opposite.

Travis wandered in and took up a position leaning against the wall behind the boy. In that position he looked like a bodyguard – he certainly seemed watchful enough. I didn't think he had much to worry about – certainly not until I'd cleaned my plate.

'What were you hunting?' asked the boy.

'What makes you think we were hunting?' I asked.

'Well, you weren't fishing, now – were you?'

'We don't know,' said Bill. 'We don't know what it was.'

I didn't tell the boy that I thought it might be a

malignant Native American spirit. I'm not stupid, and I'd been warned by Peter Grant to show some respect when dealing with the supernatural. This boy was a power – I could feel it in the way the world kept trying to wrap itself around him like a cloak.

Both Cymbeline and Peter had warned me about dealing with such people – be respectful, be careful and, above all, don't eat the food.

The trout suddenly tasted strange on my tongue. The boy must have noticed because he shot me a wide mischievous grin.

'No obligations,' he said.

'The thing we're chasing,' I said. 'Do you know what it is?'

'I can show you where it started,' he said.

'And where is that?'

'Not far,' he said. 'After breakfast.'

Then the boy stood and said something in what I realised had to be Ojibwe to Bill, who nodded and said something that was unmistakably along the lines of 'Sure, OK.'

'I'm just going to borrow your man for a bit,' said the boy, and headed out of the main room.

I looked quizzically at Bill, who shrugged and followed him out. I looked at Travis, who was collecting the plates.

'I'll wash if you dry,' I said.

It didn't even take until I'd finished the pots to get Travis's story. People who've come to terms with an old trauma often like to talk about it. To reaffirm that they *have* survived, I guess, and that they can talk about it without coming apart.

He was a vet, a former Marine who enlisted in the early nineties.

'I'd been out for three years when 9/11 happened,' he said. 'You probably remember what it was like back then. I was all fired up and ready to re-enlist. It was just a question of who with. I hadn't been a particularly good Marine, my disciplinary record was not that splendid, but I knew there was going to be a war against someone. I mean, there had to be, didn't there? Somebody had to pay. They were going to need people with training.'

'Who did you serve with?' I asked.

I'd finished the plates and started on the cutlery.

'That's where it got tricky,' he said. 'I ended up with a PMC out of Virginia. One I'd never heard of before, and for good reason. They were into some crazy stuff.'

'What kind of crazy stuff?'

'Ghosts, demons . . . witches,' he said. 'Only they had their own terminology – shades, HCPs, RCs, CCAs. These PMCs are worse than the real army for acronyms.'

'Was this Alderman Technical Solutions?' I asked.

Travis stopped mid-wipe and stared at me.

'Fuck,' he said. 'You've heard of them?'

'We've crossed paths,' I said – leaving out that I'd been dispatched to London to drag their sorry asses back to the States. The British had made it clear they didn't want to see them again on pain of sarcasm.

Travis's new career in supernatural shade suppression fell apart in Iraq.

'Fallujah,' he said.

Operation Vigilant Resolve, the First Battle of Fallujah. The VGC had deployed to follow the Marines in as they advanced into the city and deal with any shades that might have been deployed by the insurgents.

'Our intelligence' – like most veterans, Travis pronounced that word as if it were a synonym for moron – 'was that certain groups of insurgents had weaponised local shades and were leaving them behind as disrupters. Our job was to identify them and take them out.'

We'd finished the washing-up by then, but Boyd and the boy hadn't returned. Travis filled a battered black kettle and placed it on an articulated cast-iron grid and swung it over the fire.

'Coffee or tea?' he asked.

I said coffee, and asked how he and the VGC were supposed to identify these 'shades'.

'They gave us special training,' he said. 'You can sense shades if you know what to look for.'

I pushed him a little for an explanation – enough to verify that he was talking about *vestigia*, although his training had emphasised the supernatural as a threat.

'You got a kind of sixth sense about it,' he said. 'Only the more you practised the better you got. I turned out to be pretty good at it, so they made me top sniffer.'

'Let me guess,' I said. 'Because you sniffed out the supernatural.'

'My actual designation was AIS, anomalous intuition specialist, but it was always "top sniffer on point".'

'And did you sniff anything out?'

'Never got a chance,' he said. 'The advance bogged down in the outskirts. It went hand to hand. My unit got shot up in an ambush and I crawled into a culvert and stayed there until some jarheads dragged me out. Next thing I know, the VGC lost its contract and I'm heading home in coach with my pink slip, severance pay and an NDA.'

He'd gone into a depressingly predictable cycle of alcohol-fuelled decline before finding himself lying on the lakeshore just outside Ashland, with no memory of how he'd got there.

'He found me,' he said. 'Gave me breakfast and asked if I had any plans. I said "Not really", and he said, "You do now." We've been hanging out ever since.'

He stacked the last plate and dried his hands on the dish towel.

'I have bad days and good days,' he said. 'And now the good days outnumber the bad.'

The boy popped his head through the door to tell me that my clothes were dry. This seemed unlikely, but when I returned to the boy's bedroom I found them neatly piled on the bed. There was a fragrance to them, too – not unpleasant or artificial – like trees in summer. When I'd got as far as pulling my sweater on over my head, I looked up to find the boy watching me from the doorway.

'What's your relationship with Travis?' I asked.

'He was broken,' said the boy. 'He needed somewhere to heal and I needed an uncle.'

'Can he leave?' I asked. 'If he wants to?'

'That's a good question, Kimberley.' He said my name the same way my kindergarten teacher used to say it. Friendly, gentle, but with a hint of distance, so that you never forgot who was in charge of whom. 'If he went back into the world he wouldn't last a year – he'd be dead or in prison.'

'But he can leave if he wants to?'

'Any time he likes,' said the boy. 'But he knows he's much safer here with me.'

'It's not right,' I said.

'I didn't break him and then throw him in the garbage,' said the boy. 'That's all on you.'

18

The woods behind the cabin were beautiful in the sunshine. The snow glittered like spun sugar over yellow birch, hemlock and white pine. Despite the lack of a proper sleep, I felt fresh and clean. Even the cold was invigorating.

Travis led us through the woods until we reached a proper path. It was wide and well used enough to be visible even with a foot of snow on top. There was a National Park trail marker near where we joined the path. Hanging by a piece of string from the top of the marker was a letter-sized piece of white paper inside a clear plastic filing wallet. Printed in a huge font were the words DANGER: TRAIL CLOSED.

Travis nodded at the sign.

'He had me reroute the paths the hikers take,' he said. 'But you shouldn't have any trouble finding the location.'

'Is it marked?' I asked.

'No,' he said. 'But you'll know when you're getting close.'

And then he turned and tramped back into the woods. I fumbled a scrap of torn paper out of my pocket and slipped it into the plastic folder. That way we'd know where to get off the trail on the way back.

'Good thinking,' said Bill.

Travis had been right – I did know when I was getting close. There was a rising dread in the centre of my chest, a prickling of the hairs on my arms and a smell like cold metal.

'Can you feel that?' I asked Bill.

'Feel what?' he asked.

'Dread, fear . . . something.'

He turned and gave me a questioning look, and then frowned.

'Is this that magic thing you talked about?'

'Yes,' I said.

He nodded to himself and looked left and right, and then pointed off the path to the left.

'Over there?' he asked.

'Yeah,' I said – there was a definite creepy vibe coming from the left.

We left the trail and started working our way through the trees. The ground was uneven and we were forced to climb down into a gully at one point. Travis had given us a packet of red ribbons to mark our route every twenty feet or so, and strict instructions to collect them all up on our way out.

It was hard to square the growing unease I felt with the pristine wilderness around us, but it wasn't long before we reached the shore. Here, a section of sandstone cliff had fallen away to reveal an entrance into a cave. Stone and earth had slid down into the darkness, creating a makeshift ramp.

It looked dark and treacherous, but dark and

treacherous is my profession. Plus we'd brought some propane lamps with us. Even so, the footing was dangerous and patches of ice clung to the rocks beneath our feet. The walls glowed a sandy brown and red in the lamplight, and seemed composed of thin layers piled on top of each other.

Bill took off his right glove and brushed his fingertips along the wall.

'Sandstone, I think,' he said. 'But it's been a while since college geology.'

As we descended, I became aware of a rotting smell – plant or animal matter or mould in the process of decomposing. It got strong enough that it almost overwhelmed the cold dread that emanated from the depths of the cave. Almost.

'Can you smell that?' I asked.

'Yes,' said Bill, which meant it probably wasn't a *vestigium*. 'Something died recently.' He coughed. 'Not that recently, I think.'

The entrance tunnel opened up into a round chamber thirty feet across, with a domed roof that peaked twenty feet above a shallow dish-shaped floor. My geology was even further back than Bill's, but the cave seemed far too regularly shaped to be natural. Certainly the erosion on the cliffs outside had created sharp horizontal blades of rock where layers had eroded away at different speeds. In the cave the walls were smooth, as if sanded down to bring out the grain.

'My brain keeps saying Precambrian, which makes this almost a billion years old,' said Bill.

'I thought college geology was a long time ago?' I said.

'Some things stick,' he said. 'And paleoclimatology is a rapidly growing field.'

Once we were safely down the rockslide, we stood where we were and looked around.

The floor of the cave was littered with corpses.

Bureau agents work surprisingly few murders, at least not directly. Mostly we work white-collar or organised crime, and even the Behavioral Science Unit tends to work at one remove. Processing a crime scene is usually handled by local law enforcement. We definitely learn the basics, though, and one of the things we're trained to consider is whether what we're looking at is a crime or archaeology.

It can be both – of course.

I counted three bodies at the base of the rockslide. They were brown, with scraps of mummified flesh and rotted fabric clinging to the major bones. They appeared complete and were laid out on their sides in a semi-fetal position – as if sleeping. I immediately thought that they were hundreds of years old, but for a used-up chemical light tube positioned by one of their skulls.

'Somebody has been down here before us,' said Bill.

'Try not to disturb anything,' I said. 'We're going to want a full CSI unit in here, and they get real pissy when you touch stuff.'

'Archaeologists, too,' said Bill.

As the only ethnographer for a hundred miles, Scott Walker had said, *you'd be surprised by what I get asked to look at.*

Walker might have been down here, but my feeling was that he was too well trained to discard his light tubes around a scene. My money was on the mysterious Mr. Bunker.

Stepping carefully around the three corpses, I picked my way over to where a fourth was sitting up against the cave wall. He was missing his skull, which had rolled off to the side, but enough of his coat had survived for me to spot tarnished silver buttons on his chest. When I squatted down for a closer look, I could make out the letters VGC embossed on each button. Lying by his side, near the skeletal remains of his right hand, was a long-barrelled single-action revolver. Probably an early Colt Paterson, which would have been the right era for the Marsh expedition of 1843. Weighed down by the pistol was what looked like a leather document pouch – remarkably intact.

This, I suspected, was Captain William Marsh of the Virginia Gentlemen's Company himself.

I turned and surveyed the cave from his point of view. From where he sat, Marsh could cover the whole area. Last stand? Had he shot down the three men in the centre, or had there been a long tense stand-off while Marsh had fought to stay awake and his former comrades waited for him to fall asleep?

How long had they been trapped down here?

Bill was squatting down on the far side of the cave. He turned and waved me over.

There was a shallow depression against one wall that extended into a sort of trench – it looked hand-dug – that extended to the left. As I approached, I felt a cold fear that had nothing to do with the outside temperature or my own emotional state – at least, I hoped not.

This was ground zero for the *vestigium* we had followed into the cave.

The depression and the trench were filled with what would be described on a forensic report as disarticulated skeletons. I counted at least five skulls, scatters of ribs and shoulder blades, hip bones, and the long bones of the arms and legs.

Bill drew my attention to a femur that lay outside the trench. There were cut marks near the joints. The memory of a couple of truly horrible seminars at Quantico rose in my mind.

'Knife wounds?' asked Bill.

'Butchery marks,' I said, and when we looked closely we could see that most of the bones had such visible cut marks.

'Well, that's horrible,' said Bill.

'At least they weren't eaten by wolves,' I said. 'That's Nanabushzoo off the hook.'

'Nanaboozhoo,' said Bill. 'And not necessarily. Somebody sealed these gentlemen in here.'

'Ordinary people could have done that,' I said. 'Throw the expedition into the cave and then keep piling on rocks until you're sure they're not going to get out.'

'There'd be stories,' said Bill. 'My uncle would have loved a story like that. Heroic tale of resistance combined with hair-raising terror. "And then they gobbled one another up." That would have been a winter story, for sure.'

'It might have been forgotten,' I said. 'Deliberately forgotten, to avoid reprisals. Or it could have been done by a rival white expedition who kept it secret. Or didn't survive the winter.'

I pointed up at the hole we'd climbed in through.

'That,' I said, 'is fresh. It must have happened in the last year. I can't believe Ms Clarkson would have found this location and left that document pouch.'

I indicated back where Captain Marsh stood guard over his documents, and Bill stood to get a better look. As he held up his lamp, the shadows shifted in the bone pit, revealing that somebody – or something – had been digging out the centre.

'And Patrick Henderson wouldn't have disturbed the scene this badly,' I said.

'Our mysterious Mr. Bunker?' said Bill, returning to squat down beside me.

The bones in the depression did look disturbed – recently disturbed – as if someone had unceremoniously pulled them out of the depression and piled them either side. Among the discarded bones was another expended chemical light. Somebody had definitely dug down through the bones to the bottom of the depression.

Gingerly, I reached down and cleared away what I recognised as the small bones of the hand. As I did, the dreadful cold that wasn't really there intensified until I was sure that, despite my gloves, the tips of my fingers were blackening with frostbite.

There was a rectangular hole dug into the bottom of the depression, six inches long, three inches wide and five inches deep. Something had been buried there, something that radiated a *vestigium*, and something that I was sure had been removed fairly recently.

Three guesses as to by whom.

We moved away from the butcher pit and I found

myself unconsciously clamping my hands under my armpit, trying to lose that ghostly chill.

'Are we going to open the folder?' he asked.

'I think we must,' I said.

But we were careful, and I temporarily swapped my cold weather gloves for the latex pair I always carry.

Inside was a leather-bound journal like that of Ephraim Wright, only this one's pages were glued together and I didn't dare force them. Less damaged was a hand-drawn map of the local shoreline and the nearest Apostle Islands. Few inland features had been mapped, but the curve of Eloise Bay was obvious, as was Eloise Point, although neither were labelled as such. North of the point where the hotel stood, an X had been drawn with the letters *WCDec1843* above.

'That confirms the location of the Winter Camp,' said Bill. 'Ada will be pleased. Once she's rebuilt, she can use that on her website.'

South of Eloise Point, just back from where I judged the marina to stand in the present day, a pair of offset triangles had been drawn. When I squinted, I saw they were supposed to be wigwams.

'Goddamn tipi,' said Bill. 'Even back then they couldn't tell the difference between a tipi and a wigwam.'

'That's the village,' I said, and Bill huffed unhappily.

Underneath the village, written in a different hand, spikier and with a definite slant to the left, was *EVUH Ps.149.7*.

Psalms Chapter 149, line 7. I was pretty fair at Bible study, but it took me a moment to summon up the verse.

'To execute vengeance upon the heathen and punishments

upon the people,' I said, and Bill gave me a questioning look. 'I only remember it because I had to ask what a heathen was.'

'I think we know who they were in this instance,' said Bill.

19

We took the leather document pouch, but left everything else the way we'd found it – even the expended chemical lights. It might not be an active crime scene, but it was still of enormous historical importance, and definitely a grave site.

Bill stayed quiet as we returned to the trail and then found our way back to the cabin. As we had been instructed, we removed the ribbons as we went. I wasn't worried. Once an assessment team had been assembled it would be easy enough to locate the cave from the air.

The farther away from the cave we got, the more the feeling of cold fear thankfully subsided, until it began to feel like something I had imagined or seen on TV. Without it, I found I could think more clearly and start to develop a working theory of the crime.

If it was a crime, rather than a natural disaster or a historical incident.

Something – possibly rumours of interesting magic – had brought Sadie Clarkson, verified magical practitioner, up from the Crescent City to sleepy Eloise. There, either by coincidence or design, she had met up with Patrick Henderson, former agent and keen local historian. Between them they discovered the Ephraim Wright journal that confirmed that Marsh had been lured away from his winter camp by a young Native boy.

I couldn't help thinking of the nameless boy waiting for us back at the cabin. Peter Grant had briefed me once that even if a *genius loci* died, there could be continuity between the old spirit and any new spirit that took over later.

I was going to have come back and ask questions. But right now I had more immediate concerns.

Given that Scott Walker, the BIA's magic man on the spot, hadn't known about the journal, I was certain that Clarkson and Henderson had tried to keep its existence secret. Nonetheless, whoever Mr. Bunker had worked for had learned the journal's content, and he'd arrived in the fall to start looking for the Marsh Expedition's last resting place. Staying at the hotel had been a smart move. That way, he'd been starting each search from the exact location of the winter camp. At some point he obtained an inflatable and expanded his search to the nearest Apostle Islands.

I was almost certain that it was Mr. Bunker who'd located the cave and then removed something from underneath the charnel pit – a rectangular box-shaped thing six inches long. Something that gave off such a powerful *vestigium* that it contaminated both the cave it had been hidden in and the boathouse back at the hotel.

Mr. Bunker had made it back to the boathouse, at least, before something had caught up with him and dragged him away leaving only his cell phone, the remains of the inflatable and his severed arm behind.

My money said the snow monsters were aiming to

recover what Mr. Bunker had removed from the cave.

But that must have happened before the lake froze, or else how did he get back across the water?

'Bill,' I said, 'when did the lake between here and Eloise freeze enough to be impassable to boats?'

'Five days ago,' he said. 'Although it wouldn't have been safe to walk on.'

The day Patrick Henderson had called the Bureau. So why had the snow monsters come looking for Patrick Henderson and, later, why had they attacked the hotel? Scott Walker had been convinced that they were after him. Had he known something that he didn't tell me? Scratch that – of the many things Walker hadn't wanted to tell me, did one relate to the snow monsters?

Something had been taken from the cave, something so powerful that it left a *vestigium* over a wide area. Had Mr. Bunker passed it on to Walker? Did he have it with him while we were in the hotel, and then later at the library? Was that why Two Heads and the snow monsters had gone after him, rather than me?

All right, it wasn't so much a theory of crime as a set of questions from *Jeopardy* . . .

We needed to get back to Bayfield before the answer became 'widespread loss of life'.

And I needed to phone a friend – even if that was the wrong metaphor.

The latter was easy. The cabin had a satellite dish, and when I asked the boy if he had an internet connection to go with it, he laughed.

'How else am I supposed to play GTA online?' he said.

He led me into the cabin's main room and dug out a handset that provided a connection that didn't rely on local cell phone coverage.

I couldn't reach Agent Doughty or Deputy Larson, but I did raise the FBI office in Wausau, who informed me that Doughty had obtained some snowmobiles to get over the southern pass. They asked for my current location, and when I told them they wanted to know how the heck I'd got there.

'It wasn't easy,' I said, and then gave them as detailed a report as I dared, to pass on to Quantico in case they didn't hear from me again. I considered calling the CIRG direct, but I was about to do something I thought that Director Lane might wish to keep himself distant from.

I had to think about the country code before I dialled the rest of the number from memory. There was that weird ringtone you get with foreign calls, then it was picked up.

'Yes,' said a voice with a British accent. 'Can I help you?'

Behind the voice I heard music, voices and the clink of glasses. Obviously I'd interrupted a night out.

'Hi, Peter, got a moment?'

'Kimberley?' said Peter. 'Sure, what do you need?'

'Got a bit of a situation here and wondered if you might have some advice.'

'Do my best,' said Peter. 'Give me a moment.'

I heard him apologise as he pushed through a crowd.

'Who are you talking to?' asked Bill.

'Scotland Yard,' I said. 'They know about this sort of stuff.'

When Peter had found a suitable spot – outside, judging by the distant traffic noise – I gave him the Grimm's fairy tale version of my adventures so far – including the sense impressions that were definitely not going in any kind of official report.

'It sounds like a malignancy,' he said when I'd finished.

I'd heard of those, although my sources were vague beyond the notion that they were places of great evil and one should avoid building housing on them. Cymbeline once called it spiritual pollution – like industrial contamination, only supernatural. I didn't think that could be a coincidence.

'Have you ever encountered one?' I asked.

'Apart from vampires, only a small one in Kew Gardens,' he said. 'We dealt with that with a combination of weedkiller and white phosphorus. Can you wait half an hour while I check some of this with Nightingale?'

I said I could, and he hung up.

I realised that the boy was standing right beside me – I hadn't heard him come in.

'So,' said the boy. 'Was that London?'

I said it was.

'Are you talking to the Nightingale or the Starling?'

Peter had warned me about these nicknames, and the tendency of people in the demi-monde to stick the definite article on people. Peter had joked that people probably referred to me as 'the Agent', but so far nobody had done it in my hearing.

'The Starling,' I said. 'How do you know about them?'

'There is a little bird from London called the Crane

who never stops travelling. She loves to fly from place to place, and wherever she lands she tells wonderful stories. And her price for telling you a story is that you tell her a story in return. She was here last fall. Came and told stories at the school.'

'You go to school?'

'Bayfield High,' he said. 'Go Wolverines. You thought I lived here full-time? I stay with a nice old couple and take their name for school enrolment.'

'Do they know who's sleeping under their roof?' I asked.

'They lost their son and their grandchildren five years ago,' said the boy. 'I only just found them in time. They were this close . . .' he held up his hand, thumb and forefinger half an inch apart, 'to taking some pills and going to sleep forever.'

I thought of Travis.

'More broken lives?' I asked.

'The land is broken, the world is unfair, and the innocent suffer terrible blows,' said the boy. And then he smiled, and I felt the warmth of him like the sun rising over a spring pasture. 'I can't fix everything, so I do the best I can.'

'In that case, can I borrow your snowmobile?'

'No,' he said sweetly. 'But only because I've got something better.'

He bounded out of the front door and I watched him from the window as he spoke to Travis. The big man nodded and headed off toward the shed, and I saw that Bill was standing nearby, hood thrown back, staring up into the sky. Much as he'd been when I'd first seen him outside the demolished town hall. He looked over as the boy called his name and walked over to join him. I remembered our make-out session and my lips actually tingled. I wondered at the fabulous inappropriateness of reverting to my freshman self in the middle of a case.

'Where were you, Bill,' I said to the window, 'when I had all that free time in college?'

And as if they'd heard me, both Bill and the boy turned to look at me. I gave a pathetic little wave that Bill returned with a smile, and the boy gave me a knowing look. They resumed their conversation, and Bill said something that made the boy laugh and shake his head.

I stepped smartly away from the window and waited for Peter to call me back.

Which he did five minutes later.

'I've got good news and bad news,' he said. 'Which do you want first?'

'I'll take the bad news.'

'If they're allowed to get big – the term the books use is "fester" – then they can have a major impact on the local environment. That could explain your mutant deer and maybe the weather, too.'

Somebody young and female said something in the background. I couldn't make out the words, but she sounded exasperated.

'We're not sure about the weather,' said Peter. 'Abigail believes the amount of energy required to alter the weather is too high.'

Another interjection from Abigail.

'Could you send us any observations you might make along the way?'

You're in luck, I thought, *I have a genuine meteorologist in tow. If both of us make it out, he can give you a full report.*

'I'll see what I can do,' I said. 'What's the good news?'

'There's always a single point – a core, if you like,' he said. 'If you find that and destroy it, preferably with fire, the whole malignancy collapses.'

'Kill it with fire,' I said. 'Right. How much fire?'

'Do you have access to incendiary grenades?'

Unfortunately the DLA's 1033 Program didn't stretch that far – so I asked if there was an alternative.

'An accelerant, and lots of it,' said Peter. 'Petrol, diesel, whatever you can get. The fire is important – it doesn't have to be fast, it just has to be thorough.'

I thanked Peter and hung up.

If the heart of the malignancy wasn't at the cave, then I had a horrible suspicion I knew where it had gone. Or rather – who was carrying it around. I checked the load-out on my pistol and pulled on my parka. I was zipping it up when Bill walked back inside. While he gathered his own gear, I asked what the boy had said and Boyd shrugged.

'He said that I had no obligation to help,' he said. 'That it wasn't my problem and I should leave the solving of it to those who had created it in the first place.'

'By that, I suppose he meant me?'

'You and all the other white people,' he said.

'What did you say?'

'I said that I had to know the truth.'

'Is that what made him laugh?'

Boyd hesitated and looked away.

'Yeah,' he said. 'Totally.'

*

We left the boy at the top of the steps and walked down to the iced-up cove. There, Travis was preparing a dogsled. This was our better alternative to the snowmobile.

'That makes sense,' said Bill. 'Less ground pressure.'

I glanced back up at the top of the cliff, but the boy was gone.

Travis finished laying out the traces, looked back toward the island and whistled. Immediately, four grey-brown shapes came bounding out of hiding and ran toward him. I assumed at first they were huskies, but they seemed too big and their snouts too pointed.

'Those are huskies, right?' I asked Bill.

'Those are not huskies,' he said, keeping his voice low.

'What are they, then?'

'They're not wolves,' said Bill, as the canines lay down in formation so that Travis could attach them to the traces.

'How do you know?'

'Because wolves don't pull dogsleds.'

Travis finished harnessing the things that were definitely not wolves and walked back to the driving position.

'You two shouldn't sweat the details so much,' he said, and then nodded at the sled. 'All aboard.'

Bill climbed in first and I sat down between his legs. The rearmost not-wolf turned to look over its shoulder at us. It had intelligent yellow eyes and I could swear it was smiling. Certainly there were plenty of teeth on display. I felt Bill's arms tighten around me.

'Nothing to worry about,' I said.

Travis climbed into the driving position and gripped the handles.

'If you gentlemen would be so kind,' he said to the four in the traces.

The . . . let's call them 'canines' took off – fast. I've been in jet planes that accelerated less quickly.

As we gained speed, the sled seemed to rise until it ran on top of the snow, until we were gliding smoothly and quietly – as if we were flying. Even with the amazingly wolf-like huskies kicking snow in my face, I found myself caught up in the excitement and joy of the moment.

This is how Saint Nick feels every Christmas, I thought, *no wonder he's so jolly.*

20

Accord to Bill, Eloise was less than two miles across the ice – an eternity when we were on foot, but ten minutes by dogsled. The far shore, which had seemed so distant when we were at the cabin, was suddenly immediate and close.

The sky had cleared over the town and I could see Eloise Point, and beyond that the houses rising up the slope behind the marina. Sunlight flashed on glass and a moment later we heard the unmistakable clatter of helicopter blades. One rose from the marina, small, civilian, and painted red and white.

'Looks like your backup has arrived,' said Bill in my ear.

I grinned, but right on cue, trouble arrived.

There was an outbreak of snarls and howls from the traces as the canines felt it first, but I sensed it soon after. A terrible sense of violence and anger coming from behind me, like the baying of a lynch mob.

I twisted awkwardly so I could look over Bill's shoulder.

A plume of white was erupting out of the ice less than a hundred yards away. Even as I watched, it began to twist and rise. Chunks of shattered ice were spinning up around its base and catching the sunlight as they flew away. A piece the size of a kitchen table whipped over our heads and crashed down ahead of the sled.

The canines snarled and swerved around it.

I looked back again and saw that it was a full-blown twister that rose into a cloudless sky. If you know anything about tornados at all, you know that they don't rise up from the ground, and they don't happen without an accompanying storm.

'There's no mesocyclone!' shouted Bill. 'That had better be down to magic, or otherwise we can kiss goodbye to the laws of thermodynamics.'

'They'll have to rewrite all the textbooks,' I said, marvelling at how calm I was given the circumstances.

'Nah,' said Bill. 'The science has to be obsolete for at least twenty years before they do that. Forty years, if we're talking about Texas.'

'It's following us,' I said.

Really big tornados can travel up to a hundred miles an hour, but the small ones crawl along in the high twenties. Still, faster than a dogsled. Even one drawn by canines of indeterminate parentage.

Travis glanced over to see where we were looking, and swore. He turned his attention back to the definitely not wolves.

'If you could pick up the pace, boys,' he called. 'We seem to be on the clock.'

The snarls and howls died away and there was a sudden surge of acceleration. I had no idea how fast we ended up going, but the ice tornado started to fall behind. Ahead, I could see figures moving around on the marina; the town plough and backhoe were yellow and red boxes.

They must have used them to clear an LZ for the helicopter. They'd positioned it in front of a building I recognised as the emergency shelter.

I lost sight of it as we entered the harbour and the pier obscured my view. Then the sled racketed up the same slipway to the ice road that Bill and I had raced down the previous night. Then it turned sharply, the rear skidding around behind the canines, and we were running along the waterfront road.

A heavily armed group of men and women in camouflage, body armour and advanced combat helmets were milling around in front of the emergency centre. They might have been state troopers, National Guard, or even local deputies. After 25 years of the military equipment reutilisation programme, it can be hard to tell them apart – especially since many small departments don't even bother to dye the camouflage blue.

They jumped out of the way fast enough when Travis drove the sled up beside the LZ, and Bill and I unceremoniously rolled off and scrambled to our feet.

'If you would be so kind!' shouted Travis, and the sled shot off, scattering the – at a guess – state troopers on their way out.

'FBI,' I shouted, and hauled out my badge to wave at them. 'FBI!'

'University of Wisconsin,' called Bill, and then quieter in my ear, 'My ID was in the truck. Do you think that will be a problem?'

Before I could answer, somebody called my name.

'Agent Reynolds?'

A man in a blue puffer jacket with an FBI badge hanging on the outside strode toward me. He was built like a linebacker, and his hood was thrown back to reveal a square head with grey eyes and unnecessarily cropped sandy hair.

'Agent Doughty?' I said. 'Am I pleased to see you.'

A couple of paces behind Doughty came Scott Walker. He had a red gym bag over his shoulder, but there was something about the way he kept his hand on it – as if he expected an assailant to try and snatch it at any moment. When he was less than six feet away, I felt a wave of cold fear wash over me, and I knew what was in the bag.

'Are you injured?' asked Agent Doughty. 'We have another bird inbound in five. The BIA wants an immediate evac.'

He jerked his head at Walker, who was hanging back and trying to look inconspicuous.

I was about to step over and have words with him when Bill clutched my arm.

'Kimberley,' he said. 'Look.'

I turned and looked.

The ice tornado was less than two hundred yards from the marina, a funnel of dirty white that had gathered a swirling mass of slate-grey cloud at its top. Bill's missing mesocyclone – I hoped he was happy.

'Oh, shoot,' I said, which provoked a snorting cough of a laugh from Bill. I turned back and got Agent Doughty's attention.

'Wave off the bird,' I told him, and watched as his

eyes flicked to the tornado and back to me. 'Clear everyone out of here. Go north, away from the town, and find shelter.'

I will always have a special place in my heart for Agent Doughty, because after a short pause, he didn't argue or second-guess me. Instead, he spun around and started shouting instructions.

I located Walker again. When he saw me bearing down on him, he took an involuntary step backward and clutched at the gym bag.

'No,' he said. 'I have to get this clear. Don't you understand?'

'Give me the bag, Walker,' I said. 'That has to be destroyed right now.'

'Are you mad?' he asked, and he seemed genuinely perplexed.

I heard a falsetto scream to my right and the distinctive sound of an M4 carbine being fired in bursts of three. I whirled and saw that one of the state troopers had stopped running and had opened fire. I turned farther to see at what — and felt a shock of fear that had nothing to do with whatever it was Walker had in the gym bag.

The ice tornado had reached halfway along the pier. Black bits of debris were whirling around the funnel, which was now collapsing, squashing down into a slower-spinning but bulbous shape, while the clouds above it ran ahead and loomed over us like a slow-motion tidal wave.

But that wasn't what had spooked the state trooper.

Emerging from the base of the funnel was a humping,

flailing mass of glistening green, red and black. From the front of it emerged thick ropey tentacles that whipped forward, groping blindly ahead.

Maybe it was finding dry land heavier going than the ice, but it had slowed to a slow jog – which was still fast enough to scare me spitless. I was amazed only one trooper had opened fire. I was going to shout for him to cease and get clear when Agent Doughty, getting himself another Kimberley Reynolds merit award, seized the trooper by the back of his flak jacket and dragged him away.

There was a flash and the sound of thunder, and Bill grabbed my hand and pulled me toward the town. Walker was already running away, heading for the emergency centre. Something hard smacked me in the shoulder and I stumbled. Hail the size of golf balls started plopping into the snow all around us.

'You've got to be fucking kidding me,' said Bill.

And then the clouds descended and we were running through a thick fog. The building housing the emergency centre was a rectangular shadow ahead, its open door a rectangle of yellow light. I saw a figure – Walker – run inside. And the door closed behind him.

I flattened myself against the wall beside the door and motioned to Bill to do the same on the other side. Luckily, he'd watched enough TV to know what I wanted and stepped to one side. I paused to take stock.

It was utterly quiet and I couldn't see more than five feet in any direction. Looking over at Bill I could see moisture beading on the hood and shoulders of his parka. He looked back at me and gave a little shrug – what now?

I drew my pistol and took a deep breath.

Either Walker was so far gone that he would shoot me as I breached, or he wasn't. Or maybe he'd gone out the back way and was running up Main Street. That would be the sensible thing.

There was a noise from the direction of the marina, like a huge belly slithering across tarmac and then snow. I saw a whipping elongated shadow writhing out of the fog and decided that the time for assessment was over.

'When we go in,' I said quietly to Bill, 'I want you to grab whoever is in there and get them out the back door.'

He frowned.

'I'll deal with Walker and be right behind you.'

The frown deepened.

'I promise.'

The slithering stopped and a low moan rolled out of the mist.

I pulled open the door and ducked inside.

It was much as I'd first seen it: the liquid propane space heater drying a line of damp clothes; trestle tables crowded with gear and boxes and food wrappers. Deputy Larson, in a forest green parka, was standing in front of the space heater, holding her unzipped parka open to catch the heat. Walker was standing back aways by the tarpaulin-shrouded boat where the spare LP bottles were kept. He still had his left hand clutched into the fabric of the gym bag.

Deputy Larson was telling him that they expected the road up to Red Cliff to be cleared within the hour. I didn't think he'd bothered warning her about the gigantic slime monster heading her way.

As soon as he saw me, Walker yanked his pistol free and aimed it at me. A sloppy one-handed grip, because he refused to let go his grip on the gym bag. I nearly shot him out of pure reflex, but his life was saved by my training. I didn't need to think about my own weapon, only Walker's intent. I made a judgement call and kept my pistol pointing down.

Larson hesitated and then drew her own gun, looking between Walker and me, obviously hoping for a clue as to who the bad guy was.

'Deputy Larson,' I said in the calm *I am a G-man* voice you pick up from your instructors at Quantico, 'there's another tornado heading right for us. I need you to take Mr. Boyd to safety.'

I flicked my eyes at Boyd and he closed the gap with Larson.

'It's a category two,' he said. 'And we're right in its path.'

Larson glanced in the direction of the marina, at me, at Walker, and then finally at Boyd, who nodded encouragingly.

'We need to go now,' he said.

'What about . . .?' she asked.

'We'll be right behind you,' said Walker unexpectedly – which seemed to settle Larson, and she led Bill out the rear door of the shelter.

'Drop the bag, Scott,' I said, keeping my pistol lowered but taking a step closer.

'You don't understand,' he said.

'Scott, it's pure evil,' I said, and even as I said it I

could feel the dreadful spiritual coldness coming off the bag like waves. How could Walker stand it?

'Yes, of course it is,' he said.

And his aim steadied, forcing me to stop shuffling forward.

'And it's a weapon,' he said.

'Against who?'

'The spirits of this land,' he said. 'The indigenous spirits.' He shook the bag with his left hand. 'This can kill them. It can kill that!'

He jerked his chin in the direction of whatever it was approaching the other side of the wall behind me.

I hesitated, listening for something ugly and heavy to be dragging itself through the snow toward me.

'They're coming back,' he said. 'You can feel it in the quiet places and out in the mountains.'

'That's a good thing, isn't it?'

Walker's face twisted between sadness and anger and something else – something that looked a lot like grief.

'When climate change really kicks in, and there's cyclones and water shortages, who do you think is going to be better prepared?'

He was talking to himself now – it's something you get used to in law enforcement. You stop being a person; you're just a badge or a uniform, a symbol. A reflective wall that people can bounce their anger off.

'It's not going to be you metropolitans,' he said. 'What are you going to do when you can't get your avocado toast and your TikTok. They'll come off the reservations then, and they will owe us nothing – not even common decency. They'll pick off the preppers one sad little compound at a time, and with them will come the spirits of rivers, the lakes and forests. The ones we've been shitting all over for the last four hundred years.'

'Is that what you think is happening here?' I asked.

Right on cue, a heavy blow hit the marina side of the shelter, and a low howl like something dredged up from a sea monster vibrated the rafters above us.

'Don't you?' he shouted over the noise. 'It's the great spirit that the Marsh Expedition exterminated in 1844, and it is pissed.'

'No it isn't!' I shouted back.

Too late, I thought. *The spirit is back, and he's already attending high school in the next town over, and if he's after revenge it doesn't involve flattening Eloise.*

Which, I remembered suddenly, was the site not of the expedition's camp, but the Ojibwe winter village. Now it made sense – the malignancy, the ice tornado and now this return.

'Not a Native spirit,' I said. 'It *is* the Marsh expedition come back to take its revenge on the locals.'

'What?' Walker gaped at me.

'It's Marsh!' I yelled. 'Having his revenge. And he wants his fricking weapon back.'

He wasn't stupid, Scott Walker. I saw him putting two and two together, and I like to think if we had had time I could have talked him down. But the Marsh monster behind me was working to its own agenda.

I used his moment of distraction to close the gap, get inside his over-extended gun arm, hook my leg behind his knee, and down he went. Then I stomped on his wrist to make him drop his pistol and kicked it across the room.

Thump – Captain Marsh wanted in bad.

I raised my pistol, aimed and put three rounds into the spare liquid propane tanks lined up against the tarpaulin-shrouded boat. One in each tank.

Bang – and for a moment the wall bowed in slightly, and a lighting fitting by the door popped off and shattered on the floor.

Contrary to what your video game might have told you, LP tanks don't explode when you shoot them. Especially with a low-calibre pistol round. Just like gas, it needs oxygen to burn, and so you have to let it mix a bit before you get any kind of flame. How much mixing you needed, we were about to find out.

Wood splintered around the door frame as what was left of the Marsh expedition smashed its way inside. I punched Walker in the face a couple of times to daze him, so I could pull the gym bag's strap over his head. I made the mistake of grabbing the bag proper, and through the material I felt the outline of a rectangular metal box with sharp corners. Cold burned the skin of my palm even through the thick nylon. I flung the bag toward the back of the building, so that it skidded to a halt against the LP tanks.

'No,' said Walker, and tried to twist and crawl after the bag. 'We need that.'

I had to stop myself from pummelling him some more, and instead I hauled him to his feet.

The wall collapsed and the monster started to squeeze itself inside. It thrashed and squirmed – trying to get a tentacle through the hole. And still Walker tried to wriggle free and run for the bag.

'As God is my witness, Scott,' I shouted, 'if you do not come with me now, I will shoot you where you stand!'

He turned to stare at me, wild-eyed, then at the creature that was filling the hole it had made in the wall. A slash opened and yawned wide, revealing a wet red interior lined with sharp white teeth.

Walker bolted for the rear and I, pausing only to turn the LP heater so that it faced toward the back door, followed on at a sprint speed I probably hadn't achieved since high school.

I turned in the doorway and took a moment to take up a proper two-handed firing stance and take a couple of deep breaths.

The creature had dragged more of itself inside, its front end swaying left to right as if sniffing something out. I didn't know how long I had to wait to let the propane mix, but if the monster smashed the wall open the gas might escape.

I might have counted on the gas fire igniting the mixture on its own, thus giving me a head start. But I didn't think I wanted to risk that.

I left it as long as I dared.

I used to do fraud cases and nice simple bank robberies, I thought, and then shot the heater – right through the burner and into the tank. This time a jet of flame shot out the front. I didn't hang around to see what happened next.

This time I broke my college hundred metre record. And I'd had a track scholarship, too.

There was a disappointingly muted *whumph* sound behind me, and a wave of heat struck my back. Firelight glittered off the waist-high snow bank that had been thrown up by recent ploughing. I half-jumped, half-fell into the cool space behind the bank and that's probably what saved me from serious injury.

Behind me I felt, rather than heard, it scream with rage.

It doesn't have to be fast, Peter had said. *It just has to be thorough.*

It turned out to be fast enough, because after a minute the scream choked off.

I was remarkably comfortable lying on my back in my nice shady ditch, but an indeterminate period later Bill's face appeared over the snowbank and looked down at me. He looked worried, but brightened when I told him I was all right.

'You'd better get up,' he said. 'People are asking questions.'

21

Lots of people, from the Bayfield County Sheriff's Department to Wisconsin Emergency Management, all of whom had mobilised vehicles, dogsleds and helicopters and had arrived just in time for a single FBI agent to blow up Eloise's emergency centre.

Their temper was not improved by the way the mayor and police chief of Eloise pointed out how they'd conducted their own rescue operations after a major weather disaster, with no state or federal help, and come away with only minor casualties. This proving the resilience and gosh-darn can-do spirit of true small-town America. Although I doubted they would turn their noses up at federal funds for rebuilding.

The county forensic team took one look at the rotting pile of fish and animal parts, mixed in with lake-bottom garbage, that was all that remained of the Captain Marsh monster, took samples and photographs, and then it was cleared away by the town backhoe. Nobody's camera close enough to have recorded the incident had survived, and the theory I heard was that it was garbage from the lake, picked up and deposited by a freak tornado. After an afternoon of sunshine, January weather reasserted itself with low clouds, gusty winds and sporadic snow showers.

Bill seemed a bit put out, but cheered up when he found that all the equipment – and more importantly, its data – up at Eloise Point were still intact. I wished I could have snuck off with him, but I had questions to answer. Or, put more properly – evade.

To keep both state and county officers off my back, I talked fast, threw in plenty of fed-speak and, occasionally, hid behind Agent Doughty and let him fend off questions. I did promise I'd give him a look at the case file once I was done writing it. The real case file, not the sanitised one that went into the public record.

Proving once more that information is power.

I got to prove the axiom twice more when I visited Scott Walker and Sadie Clarkson, both of whom had been medevacked to University of Wisconsin Hospital in Madison.

Bill and I caught a ride back to the city with a chatty state trooper called Pasquelle 'with an e', who regaled us with humorous traffic incident stories. I think he might have kept it up for the whole journey, only I fell asleep on Bill's shoulder after our rest stop at Spooner and then slept the rest of the way. Certainly he was still talking when he dropped us off at UW.

'That man has been doing way too many solo patrols,' said Bill.

Scott Walker wasn't very chatty – nor did he look particularly well. His left hand, where it had clutched the bag, had suffered serious tissue necrosis, and he was unlikely to regain full function. The wound itself was hidden under layers of hydrogels and pink hypoallergenic dressings.

There's a classic interview strategy that works particularly well with college-educated criminals – particularly academics. You tell them everything you know, and half the time they can't resist interrupting you to tell you where you've gone wrong.

So, leaving out Cymbeline and Mr. Bunker's files on Sadie Clarkson, I did just that. In return, Walker confirmed that he had found the 'weapon box' in Mr. Bunker's truck when it was impounded behind the town hall. One of the deputies received a small stipend in return for keeping Walker apprised of any 'hinky' incidents – which Mr. Bunker's disappearance counted as.

'I was passing through, so I stopped off at the town hall and had a look at his truck.'

'And?'

'Jeep Cherokee, ten years old, good condition, Virginia plates,' said Walker. 'I felt it as soon as I found it.'

'The *vestigium*?'

'Never felt anything like it.'

So he'd broken in and searched the truck, found the gym bag, and a separate cloth bag containing six silver dollars with a distinctive *vestigium* of their own – this one, something he'd encountered before while monitoring First People's practitioners in Canada.

'The Canadians are dangerously lax about their practitioners,' he said. 'One day it's going to come back and bite them in the ass.'

He'd taken both and secured the gym bag in the bed of his pickup, as far from the cab as possible. The coins went into his jacket, but by the time we encountered the snow monsters at the hotel, he'd lost them.

'When Ashley found her coin in the snow, I thought I might have dropped them outside the hotel.' Which explained his enthusiasm for the search.

'What do you think the significance of the coins was?'

Based on his experience in Canada, Walker thought they'd been used to seal Captain Marsh and friends into the cave. He imagined them placed in a ring around the site, preventing both Marsh and his box of evil from escaping.

'Either they lost effect over time or somebody disturbed them,' he said. 'My money is on Mr. Bunker.'

'Now I don't have to tell you that I'm going to have to write a long and detailed report for my boss in Quantico,' I said. 'So, to be frank – you left me to die, I'm completely certain of that—'

'I was prioritising the evacuation of civilians,' he said, as I knew he would.

'Of course,' I said. 'But, you know, your actions can be interpreted both ways, and I don't know about the BIA, but the Bureau takes a dim view of other federal agencies betraying their agents. So I can write up my report in one of two ways. One of which will land you in a world of hurt.'

'I think you overestimate the clout the FBI has with my people,' he said.

'I think you overestimate your value to the BIA,' I said. 'I think they would be perfectly happy to serve up your head on a plate to smooth things over. Regardless of that, down which road we travel is entirely up to you.'

'What is it you want?' he asked.

'I want open lines of communication between the magic branch of the BIA and the FBI,' I said. 'And then maybe we could avoid another situation like the one we've just had to live through.'

He nodded, thinking, and I knew he'd taken the wide, straight road of righteousness.

That wasn't the end of it, of course. But eventually we hammered out an agreement that would go up both our chains of command. We also agreed to meet back at Eloise in the spring when the lake had thawed and we could send in divers to look for the remains of Patrick Henderson, Mr Bunker and Bill's truck.

Usefully, Sadie Clarkson's room was down the hall from Walker's, but she proved to be much cagier then he was. She was sitting up and writing in a journal that she tucked under her covers when I walked in. Her face had lost most of its stiffness, but the lid of her left eye remained drooping.

I asked whether the damage was permanent.

'Brains are plastic,' she said. 'Mine will adapt around the damage, but . . .' She trailed off.

'No more magic?'

'Not if I want to be able to feed myself,' she said, and sighed.

'Let's talk federal charges,' I said, which made her laugh.

I said I was serious, which made her laugh even harder until a nurse came in and gave me a hard stare.

'OK,' I said. 'Let's talk friendly chats, maybe over coffee down in old New Orleans. You could bring some friends and we talk over issues of mutual concern.'

'Mutual concern?' said Sadie with a suddenly straight face.

'Mutual concern,' I said.

Sadie nodded and gave me a lopsided smile.

'OK,' she said. 'Coffee.'

The FBI expects you to own the cases it gives you. It doesn't matter how big, or vague, that case is – you are expected to dig in and get it done. However long it takes.

And like I said at the beginning, you get serious brownie points for generating intelligence sources.

When I came out of Sadie's room, I found Bill loitering at the nurses' station.

'I thought you'd gone home,' I said, trying not to smile too widely.

'I live on the isthmus,' he said, as if that explained everything. 'It's not far from here.'

And then we had an actual awkward silence of the sort I hadn't had for at least a decade.

'OK,' I said.

'So,' he said, 'are you hungry?'

I allowed that I might be.

'Would you like lunch?' he said. 'Coffee, tea, wine? Bar of chocolate?'

That made me laugh despite myself.

'He said I should make you laugh,' said Bill, looking pleased with himself.

'Who said?'

'The boy on the island.'

My mama says that sometimes you just have to trust

Providence and assume that the Lord knows what he's doing.

'The boy was giving you dating advice?'

Bill hesitated.

'More like relationship advice,' he said.

'And he was what? Fourteen?' I said, but a treacherous voice in my head said, *Fourteen, going on as old as the islands themselves*. 'What was his advice?'

'He said that you weren't done travelling, but if I was serious I should build you a house with a big yard that goes down to a creek. And I should fill the yard with dogs and horses—'

'Do you know anything about horses?'

'How hard can they be?' said Boyd. 'He said I should leave a lamp lit on the porch so you could find me and come visit. He said, as you finished your travels the gaps between visits would grow shorter, until one day I would wake up to find we were living together.'

'Definitely fourteen,' I said. 'And a romantic.'

'Or you could come crash at my place on the isthmus,' he said. 'Decompress before you fly back to Washington.'

'How good is your heating?'

'Very efficient, and I'll let you choose the setting on the thermostat.'

'Tempting,' I said. 'Do you have a proper bathtub?'

He grinned – he knew I was weakening

'As it happens, yes,' he said. 'A big one.'

'Then that sounds like a plan to me,' I said.

Technical Notes

Eloise is, of course, an entirely fictitious town, although Bayfield to its south and the Red Cliff Reservation to the north are real places. January 2015 saw an unusual thaw, and so the ice road from Bayfield to the Apostle Islands did not open until the end of the month.

I've taken the liberty of having the moon rise a couple of hours early, otherwise Bill and Kimberly might have been stranded on the top of Eloise Point with nothing to look at.

Likewise, eagle-eyed readers will have noticed that Reynolds describes herself as working for the FBI's Critical Incidence Response Group (CIRG), rather than the Office of Partner Engagement, as stated in *Lies Sleeping*. One can only assume that Peter had forgotten her transfer and misstated himself.

In case you're wondering, the longest single Dewey Decimal number is 331.8928292252097127430905II, and refers to the Buhler Versatile Inc. tractor company strike in Winnipeg, Manitoba, 2000–2001. The base number is: 331.8928.

Acknowledgements

I 'd like to thank the usual suspects John, Stevie and Anne for their support, Genn for the American localisation (amongst other helpful things), Adrian MacDonald for the weather, and Stacey Parshall-Jensen, sensitivity reader, diversity editor and cultural consultant.

Orion Credits

Ben Aaronovitch and Orion Fiction would like to thank everyone at Orion who worked on the publication of *Winter's Gifts*.

Agent
John Berlyne

Editorial
Emad Akhtar
Celia Killen
Sarah O'Hara

Copy-editor
Steve O'Gorman

Proofreader
John Garth

Editorial Management
Jane Hughes
Charlie Panayiotou
Tamara Morriss
Claire Boyle

Audio
Paul Stark
Jake Alderson
Georgina Cutler

Contracts
Anne Goddard
Ellie Bowker

Design
Nick Shah
Tomas Almeida
Joanna Ridley
Helen Ewing

Picture Research
Natalie Dawkins

Finance
Nick Gibson
Jasdip Nandra
Sue Baker
Tom Costello

Inventory
Jo Jacobs
Dan Stevens

Marketing
Jen McMenemy
Javerya Iqbal
Tom Noble

Production
Ruth Sharvell
Katie Horrocks

Publicity
Stevie Finegan
Leanne Oliver
Jenna Petts

Sales
Jen Wilson
Victoria Laws
Esther Waters
Group Sales teams across
Digital, Field Sales,
International and
Non-Trade

Operations
Group Sales Operations
team

Rights
Rebecca Folland
Barney Duly
Ruth Blakemore
Flora McMichael
Ayesha Kinley
Marie Henckel

Help us make the next generation of readers

We – both author and publisher – hope you enjoyed this book.
We believe that you can become a reader at any time in your life,
but we'd love your help to give the next generation a head start.

Did you know that 9% of children don't have a book of their
own in their home, rising to 13% in disadvantaged families*?
We'd like to try to change that by asking you to consider the role
you could play in helping to build readers of the future.

We'd love you to think of sharing, borrowing, reading, buying or talking
about a book with a child in your life and spreading the love of reading.
We want to make sure the next generation continue to have access
to books, wherever they come from.

And if you would like to consider donating to charities that help
fund literacy projects, find out more at www.literacytrust.org.uk
and www.booktrust.org.uk.

Thank you.

*As reported by the National Literacy Trust